Innocence Turned Deadly

Robert Duncan O'Finioan

Edited by Miranda Kelley

Second Edition

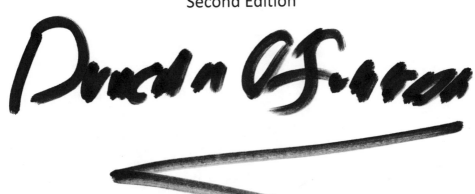

ISBN: 0615582346
ISBN-13: 978-0615582344

DEDICATION

To all the fallen Unicorns — to all the innocent victims who have lost their lives in this so called "war on drugs", a prayer I will say, my glass I will tip, your forgiveness I beg. Rest in peace.

C O N T E N T S

*"May you be in
Heaven a half
Hour before the
Devil knows
You're dead."*

— An Irish Toast

ACKNOWLEDGMENTS

To a hell of a lot of people!
You know who you are.

PREFACE

It has been ten years since the first printing of this book.

Ten *long* years. Much has happened. I finished this book after I had the now famous auto accident and MRI. Yes, those two events changed my life drastically. Damn, what an understatement!

When I first began writing this book I had very few memories of being an Omega Unit. Had never heard of something called MK ULTRA. I did not realize that I had been programmed with alternate personalities who did a lot of nasty work and left me with only gaps of missing time and no knowledge of what I had done. The car accident and the subsequent MRI triggered many of these memories to come back, but this all happened well after this book had been written.

At the time of writing this book, I had been having a huge number of re-occurring dreams that were actually memories coming out in my sleep. I can't honestly say how much influence they had on the way events are told here. I would say most likely a lot. Memories (there's that nasty word again) of being an Omega Unit were jumbled and they blurred together with the memories of working as a Unicorn. We are still trying to figure out which is which. Maybe you, the reader, will have better luck than we have had. Hey, you never know.

As I have stated previously, the names in this book have been changed to protect the guilty and you will find very few changes in this edition from the first.

'Course, if you didn't read the first you wouldn't notice, wouldn't you? Little humor guys. It's good for you.

I will tell you this as well: Everyone needs to thank Miranda Kelley for this new edition of the book, because without her faith in me and her help, you wouldn't be reading this.

You will learn more about Miranda when you read *our* book, soon to be released.

Now! Without any more babbling from me, you may indulge yourselves. Enjoy.

Robert Duncan O'Finioan

December 2010

PROLOGUE

Kentucky! I have known her all my life. At first, she was the comfort of home. Warm fires in snug houses nestled in the shadows of the gently mounded hills of Eastern Kentucky. And Inez, I am ashamed to say, is the hellhole from which I am from.

Ten years later, she was a shadow under dim streetlights, and by the time I entered my third decade of life I had an idea of what she truly was, and I pause as memories of my former life grip my throat like death coming in the black of night. At that time, twenty-one was not a time for serious self-examination — the boy still thinks he is much like Superman, and that he is immortal. I saw later that we were wrong — I was wrong.

God, if only I had a glimpse at what I know now. But alas, a boy is just a boy. Half a decade later, I felt as if I had aged fifty years. I knew Kentucky for what she really was. Kentucky was, and still is, a whore. For sale to any who has her price, and her price has always been low. Well within the reach of all who could meet the demands of her pimps, and my little hometown of Inez was and still is the lowest of the low.

Kentucky's pimps have always been the police (state and local), the sheriffs (who change in name and face only), and the judges who sat, and still sit, on her money-padded benches. Benches plush and overstuffed from deals made behind closed doors, handshakes in chambers, election favors, and the blood of the innocents.

Kentucky's largest customers have always been the coal companies that dominated the region in the east. They used and discarded the land and the people, and their sign was the dollar sign. Their heaven is a large beach house in some faraway place, paid for with blood money, dope money, and favors given them by their bought and paid for judges and politicians.

Kentucky is teeming with victims, from the coal and marijuana fields of the east, through the coke-swamped towns of Lexington, Frankfort, and the rest of the Bluegrass. Some fellow citizens have different views and opinions on this. Me, I am just telling it as I saw it.

Part of Kentucky's problem is that she is heartland. In the Bluegrass, major roadways meet and cross, and trade — dope trade and others — is always left at the crossroads. In some states, trash is barged out to sea and drowned. In Kentucky, it is elected governor, or to the bench, or sheriff, and on and on … But I digress.

This is not a novel of pure fiction. This is a fact-based tale of truth and fiction, and it will be left up to you, the reader, to (if you dare) decide what is fact and what is fiction. This is a tale of greed, corruption, lust and murder. I may have been guilty of three of the four, maybe all four. I cannot deny the greed, lust or murder. But I do not feel I was corrupt. I was fighting evil, or so I was told, and following orders. If I were corrupt then so was the system that hired me, used me, and tried so unsuccessfully to dispose of me. Like so many of those who came in contact with me. I herewith commit my story — or part of it — to the altar of public scrutiny, without apology. We did what needed to be done, despite the myth of democracy — or maybe because of it.

You may like this book, you may hate this book. However, if you read it I can promise you one thing. You will never look at a police officer of any type, or a judge, or any other elected official in the same light again.

If you are a person who can't stand to hear bad things about your government (yours, not mine), stop reading now. If you're one of those who turns a blind eye and a deaf ear to the "real" world around them, then please, put this book down now. You will not like what you read.

You will read about many things, many of them I am not proud of. You see, I fight those demons each and every day.

This is not a "make me feel good" little book. If you want that, read something else. What this book will do, or should do, is shake the living shit out of you. Or at least make you think. I wrote this book for many reasons, most of which I am keeping to myself. But one reason I will tell you is this: Revenge! Payback's a bitch, isn't it?

The Christians have a slogan: "Let he who is guiltless cast the first stone."

Picked up any rocks lately?

CHAPTER 1

A breeze rose and fell almost with our footsteps, down toward the raped stretches of land, and stirred the stench of sulfur from the invisible stream that, despite its babble, was as dead as clotted blood. Another time, perhaps, I might have shed a tear, like the Indian in the Clean Up America commercial. But tonight I was hunting, and my prey was human.

The moon-waste terrain of the strip-mined land was just ground cover, though the black water made me think of a slaughtered animal hung on a limb to be blooded. We rounded the shoulder of a blasted out boulder half as high as my head and I held up my hand as a signal to stop. There was a house in front of us about a hundred yards away and facing down the hollow, the way visitors would normally come.

This was a big house, and it had been here a long time. Not one of your dogtrot cabins, or weathered boarded-over outhouses, but an honest-to-goodness two-story house. As I studied the house sitting maybe a hundred feet below me and a hundred yards away, one of the men behind me shifted on his feet and a pebble bounced on to the solid rock of the ravine's floor. By the time it bounced the second time, we were all flat in the shadows.

The back door of the house swung open, showing us the outline of a stocky man with curly hair around his shoulders. Instead of lying still, I rattled the brush and lightly tapped my feet to make the kind of sound I hoped a deer would make.

"Nah," we heard Long Hair say to somebody behind him, "Just a damn deer. Let's get back to work."

First, though, he sent a short burst of what sounded like nine-millimeter fire high over our heads. We all got the message. This one was either slightly trigger happy or just liked the sound of full automatic fire. He went back inside, leaving the door open like the gate to Dante's Hell. Behind me, I could feel more than hear the restlessness of the Unicorn team as we waited out the obligatory minutes to be sure Long Hair didn't come back out.

We were already on our feet and moving when a second, much larger figure stepped out. Without even a glance around, he unzipped his fly and turned to the edge of the walkway. His voice was audible to us above the trickle of the ruined brook below our feet. He scratched his crotch, re-zipped his fly, stretched, yawned and disappeared again into the lighted back door of the house.

Twenty minutes later, we were in the front yard. Far away to the northwest, I could see blinking lights that might have been on a plane, or they might have been the choppers that had dropped us two miles away beyond a rugged Appalachian spur. More likely, I thought, it was the Kentucky State Police clean-up team on its way and maybe pressing us a little too closely. We hadn't made our mess yet. But the hunting looked good, and this house was our private preserve.

The sound amplifiers we wore told us two men were working away in the lower part of the house, and their conversation told us a third man was somewhere engaged in "breaking a new 'un." A new what? We did not know. It might have been a new weapon, or a new recruit. Beyond the mention of "breaking in", the only sounds we heard were snorts or grunts that didn't tell you anything unless you can read the face of the grunter.

Every now and then, their work would need their full attention, and we would hear one of them whistling softly under their breath. Then the tension would pass and snatches of "Barbara Allen" or "Lord Randall" would come to us from the older of the two voices, while the younger of the two alternated "On Top of Old Sophie" with something that began with "There ain't no grave gonna hold my body down!"

The bastards were so confident in their employer's influence that they hadn't even posted a perimeter guard. Not even a tripwire, such as one an honest mountaineer might use to protect his hen house or still, was in evidence. They were either cousins to the rum-running Kennedys of Massachusetts or they were tripping out on second-hand power. Well, before this night was over we would see about 'graves holding bodies down,' at least in this lifespan.

Now, I am about to describe an operation, or the culmination of an operation, by a group called the Unicorns. The group operated in and out of the hills of Kentucky and several other hills and cities not in the Bluegrass. Maybe they still do, I don't know.

"Unicorns," Richards, our leader, told us, "Are non-human and only half real. Beasts — each and every one of you is a beast, an animal. You got that? There ain't no room in this operation for emotion. Human involvement. Look at the man next to you. He is a killer. Don't forget it. If I tell him to, he will bring me your head on a stick! Because he is a Unicorn. And Unicorns ain't human.

"What you are going to learn is that in left-wing, bleeding heart democracies where the power belongs to the pee-oh-pul, such outfits do not exist. Repeat — do not exist! But as any sensible sociologist will tell you, there is the law, and then there is what people do. And the truth is what you can make twelve people in a jury box believe. No matter what really happened. Now, get over the idea that Jesus wants you for a sunbeam and to fart love and light, and that all men are created equal. You're going out there to play with the big boys in the real world. The animals. So, like the bumper sticker says, if you can't run with the big dogs, stay the hell on the porch."

Now here we were, more than a year later, in the front yard of a crack house somewhere on the edge of a strip-mined area in Martin County. Because when the coal went out because of high sulfur content, and with the introduction of the long-wall miner, the sleek Bell helicopters stopped ferrying men in three-piece suits and started running cocaine.

And I was running with the Big Dogs!

Our intelligence told us that one of the biggest coal companies in the world had become the biggest drug supplier in the area. Hell, in the entire Bluegrass. With connections worldwide. No one paid any attention when a company helicopter dropped into some of their ruined land. After all, they still had a lot of land to restore to contour, and many rocks were weathering out there.

We had heard that a lot of judges and state cops were retiring early and living well. But, then, this was Kentucky, where cooperation has always been a tradition. Wilkerson tried to sell the state to Spain almost before she was annexed and got a nice pension out of it. Mary Collins sold it to Japan and became a college president. I wonder sometimes if the Bluegrass ever had a chance.

However, politics was not the branch of organized crime we were concerned with that night. I waved three Unicorns around to the rear and Sean down the ground floor hall. We were well drilled and needed no spoken communication. I smiled as I kicked in the front door and sprayed the entry hall with forty-five slugs to start the rats scurrying. Above the reverberation of my machine pistol splintering the plaster was something that sounded like dry bones breaking. I saw Sean disappear down the hall shaking his head as I hit the stairs at a bound, trying to run and listen at the same time.

This was a typical Unicorn identify and destroy operation. Orders were to take no prisoners. If a company helicopter happened to drop in unscheduled, it was to crash and burn with all aboard. I don't know how the FAA investigation would have been handled, but probably unauthorized transportation of explosives would have entered into it. Mining companies do use a lot of dynamite.

Anyway, our information was that there would be three to four men processing cocaine. Once during surveillance, two girls had been flown in, then picked up the next morning. These were not small mountain town whores, nor the girls from just over the ridge. This was quality stuff. Probably from Cincinnati or Louisville, or maybe the house on North Broadway in Lexington, where University of Kentucky and Transylvania College girls are said to charge half a thousand bucks a night. I never had that kind of money to spare for that kind of amusement, so I can't swear to it (although I understand operations have been moved since the first printing of this book).

A stair creaked under my foot and sounded like thunder in my earphones. Almost at the same time, a forty-five coughed twice below and to the rear. The sound was overlapped by the higher pitched stutter of an Uzi. I felt pretty sure Long Hair had learned that it's more important to hit than just spray lead around. By the time I reached the head of the stairs, the authoritative rumble of a couple of Magnum shotguns had told me the ground floor was secure. "Barbara Allen" and "Old Sophie" had gone to rest.

At the top of the stairs, I hesitated for two or three seconds. Decision time. Two closed doors faced me with nothing to tell me which one was dangerous. As always, I thought of the Lady and the Tiger story. A magnified sound came through my earphones. I shoved them off to better orient on the noise. A sort of faint feeble scratching, like a moth's wing on paper, filtered through the door to the left.

The old fashioned surface-mounted lock flew open when I side-kicked the lock with my boot and the scene went into tableau. What I saw will haunt me until the day I die. The man was maybe forty-two or forty-three, slender and adequately muscled. The girl was maybe five or six, and she was face down on the table. Her eyes, still turning toward the sound of the splintering lock, had what might have been hope in their lost blue depths when the man drove the knife into the back of her small, helpless neck.

A glance at the smears of blood on the table and her buttocks told me she had been raped and sodomized. The rag in her mouth told me why her hands had made the only sound I had heard. By the time the arm with the knife had finished its swing, the cry "No witnesses!" reached me. "You can prove I killed her, but you can't prove I fucked her. They can't blame that one on me."

His triumph turned to puzzlement when I dropped to one knee and sent a three-round burst into his chest. Just over the heart. Then I lost it. Maybe it was those forlorn eyes over the rag-stuffed mouth. Maybe the background array of Bunsen burners and open cabinets stacked with bags of cocaine. Maybe the fact that my own daughter would soon be the age of this one. Whatever it was, this asshole would never "break in another new 'un." A red berserk rage closed over me before the dead man could finish slamming into the faded wallpaper. I remember some kind of twisted intertwined patterns of vines and flowers running up to an incongruous border of Greek frieze.

The three-round burst had killed him. The knife hit the floor before the corpse hit the wall. I began unstitching the bastard, up and down, across and back, holding the body dancing against the wall. What parts of it weren't soaking into or being imbedded in the wallpaper were flying all around the room.

I had expended maybe a dozen rounds when I kicked in the front door. Another three when I killed the bastard. An Ingram MAC-10 can take a ninety round clip, and I always used a ninety round clip when on a job such as this, so I must have hit the bastard seventy-five or so times after I killed him. As I said, the corpse was dancing on the wall and coming apart fast. Blood, brain, shit, and body matter was running down the wall. It seemed like an eternity before my bolt fell on empty.

I threw my weapon around my back on its sling and turned to the little girl, tears welling in my eyes. I began working the wadded rag out of her mouth, then pressing my hand to the wound in her neck while I fumbled for a handkerchief. Somehow, she managed to take hold of my hand, hope still in her eyes as they glazed over and her gurgling breath stopped.

I lost it again. Still holding the little body in one arm, I pulled my weapon back to the front and detached the magazine. I had decided to shoot the bastard some more. So I laid the small, lifeless body back on the table. I was still fumbling with a fresh magazine when Richards stalked into the room, his face placid behind a cloud of cigar smoke.

"What the hell is wrong with you?" I heard him say as three other Unicorns trotted in behind him. I whipped the MAC-10 up and squeezed the trigger as I pointed it at Richards. The gun was still empty, and I didn't even have the satisfaction of hearing the hammer fall on an empty chamber as the other Unicorns grabbed me from all sides and wrestled it away from me. Richards turned away from me and waved his cigar around the room. "Log it and get the hell out of here." He was as unruffled by the corpse and the splattered body as he was by my attempt to kill him — one cold son of a bitch. A true animal.

Not so were Kentucky's finest, the state police who were sent to clean up. Wherever you looked there was a state cop heaving his guts up. I guess their training had failed to prepare them for follow-up operations here, where the clean-up was done with a shovel and bucket.

Anyway, their job was to dispose of the bodies and drugs, and dummy up a story like how a prisoner or two was taken then turned over to authorities in some far off state on a fugitive warrant or something. From all the Bunsen burners and other equipment in use, the house might have been hooked into one of the dozens of gas wells in the area, and I half expected to see the house go up in flames from an open gas line. I don't know if it happened. An hour from the time I first saw the house, and less than ten minutes after I kicked in the first door, I picked up my spent magazine. Sean handed me my Ingram as I walked out of the yard. I didn't look back.

Halfway down the rough leveled half-acre that served the coal company crack factory as a heliport and parking lot, Sean stumbled over a loose rock. When he righted himself, he was chuckling. "You really would have shot our Ernst, wouldn't you?" he asked as he draped an arm across my shoulders.

"What do you think?" I asked him, as I flicked my flashlight where the Blackhawks and Cherokees were waiting. They were too far away for the beam to reach, but at least we wouldn't have to climb up the hundred feet of rope to get a ride back to debriefing. Richards probably didn't want any blood or brain matter smudged on those neat nylon ropes. "Sean, my friend, did you ever feel like you couldn't kill something enough and just shooting it somehow fell short in punishment?" I asked, as we picked up our pace.

"Ever since I was a kid," Sean answered. "When I was about eight years old I had a hamster, a golden hamster. Just a white-bellied rodent, no bigger than my hand is now."

Big friggin' hamster, I thought to myself.

"Uh, Sean," I said. "I've heard this one before."

"Quiet, lad," came his reply. "You need to hear this. Now where was I? Ah, yes. This hamster was a super hamster. He had to be strong because he learned to spread the bars of his cage and get out. Every night he would wake me up, snuggling against my shoulder.

"Well, my older sister had a kitten, a mean half-Siamese sumbitch that would rake his claws across any ankle he could get to, except Margaret's. One morning I realized Clark hadn't woken me up. I called him Clark Kent, and I found him at the door to my room. That slant-eyed bastard kitten was sitting there with his paws hooked out waiting for Clark to move. Despite being wet with cat saliva, the little body was still faintly warm. So the cat played with him, maybe for hours. Probably crippled him first so he couldn't get away. Then he came back and played with him.

"Of course," he continued on, "I couldn't kill the cat … then. My sister ran out of her room, grabbed him up, and ran to Mama for protection. You know what reminded me of Clark Kent? It was that baby lying on that table. Played with then killed. I suppose the prick thought he was going to get to be tried, and one of those hill juries would go easier on a murder than they would on rape and sodomy of a child."

He was right, of course. These old boys may not put too high a value on life, but they sure do on self-respect and dignity. No one ever said they were the brightest people on earth.

"Anyway, I buried Clark Kent in a shoe box, and then I went back behind the garage and dug a hole big enough to hold a hat box. I wanted to bury that damn cat alive, but he would have ripped my hands open and left evidence my sister would have recognized. I wound up smashing him with the flat side of a shovel and cramming him into a small hat box."

By now, we had reached our Jeep Cherokee. The Blackhawks were for Richards and the state police. The other Unicorns were catching up to us. "As far as my sister ever knew, old Sun Yat Sin just wandered off. But my daddy would look at me sometimes and rub the scars on his ankles. Times I'd swear he tipped me a wink, but I did my best to look puzzled."

Sean paused and fished out one of the long brown cigarettes he favored. "My point, Duncan, is that what you felt up there is older and more basic than any concept of justice man ever came up with, my friend. Christ may have died for our sins, but that can't match the satisfaction we feel from putting a few rounds of lead into some asshole that is feeding off the young and weak-minded. And you know by now, money is a great insulator. No matter how you get it, it protects you from the slings and arrows of outraged justice. The only thing you have to worry about is vengeance, and our Christian laws have outlawed that. Our only hope for real justice is the sort of end-run we are giving the pricks, where you shove a muzzle up their ass and run through a magazine.

"Hang in there. That kid could have been your own little girl, could she not? Same hair, same eyes. Only one thing wrong with your actions. You didn't stay cool. Get hot later and scream like hell. But keep your cool while the action is on. And Duncan, I think you really would have shot Richards. You scared that man tonight. You scared me, too."

"You really need to grow eyes in the back of your head, my boy," he added.

I shoved the empty magazine back into the action of my Ingram, and swung up into the Cherokee. I'd have rather been piloting the jeep over the rocky and potted roads to give me something to occupy my mind, but debriefing would have to come first. I settled down for some long and useless thoughts while the rest of the five-man team gave me an occasional glance. All but Sean, who I swear was asleep before the jeep pulled out. That ever lovin' bastard.

CHAPTER 2

Behind us, I supposed the Kentucky State Police had finished puking and started whatever operation they routinely did after one of our "surgical procedures," as Richards occasionally referred to the hits. I was going over in my mind the whole operation: from the swaying chopper down the two hundred feet of rope and into the pines and sweet gums. The two-mile hike seemed like two hours of wasted time, considering the security the house had. We might as well have set down on the roof and chopped our way through with fire axes. That's an exaggeration of course, but the cautious stalking had been a total waste this time.

Other times it hadn't been, and we never knew when we were going up against a new group who was as scared of the coal company as they were of us — and cautious, accordingly. Let me explain here. Sometimes a man would get a few thousand dollars ahead and rush off to Florida to grab a half-key or key of cocaine. Say seven thousand for a half-kilo or ten thousand for a full key. Whether he flies it up in a Cessna or drives it up in a beat up Chevrolet, it's worth thirty thousand when it gets back to Kentucky — before it's cut for street sale.

By this time, it's become a real hot potato. If the politicians don't get their cut, you have the state police to reckon with, and some of them are running their own game on the side with state seed money.

It works this way: the state police finance a dealer who goes to Florida to make a buy, the dealer turns his ten thousand seed money into thirty thou in a quick wholesale turnover. By the third turnover, he's holding a quarter mil, and splits with his trooper backers. Maybe by now the super troopers (not to be confused with Super Soldiers) who aren't profiting are demanding action. They're told the investigation is continuing. Arrests are expected to be made shortly because, when you're using state funds to finance an illegal operation — a crime — you have to show results.

Let me explain the solution. But please bear with me. This is, after all, government work we are talking about here. Every nine months to a year, the operation turns into a genuine sting. The dealer supplies a small amount, say a few ounces of street-grade cocaine, to some amateur who wants to get quick money, and passes the word. The super troopers make the arrest and everybody is happy. Especially the dealer and his state police buddies. A dealer is off the streets, even if he never touched the stuff before.

Or maybe the dealer just hires some poor dumb son of a bitch to make a delivery. This will be somebody who's been taken to one of those coke parties and been flattered by having a governor or ex-governor pointed out to him. And by being allowed to count hundred-dollar bills till his thumb gets tired. Anyway, he never suspects that the guy who's carrying sixty-eight thou in cash and another ninety in coke is setting him up (and believe me, the state boys are some of the best at setting people up). When he makes his delivery, guess who's waiting? You win the fur lined slop jar if you guess your ever-loyal, ever-loving state police. Again, the sucker gets five to eight in the state penitentiary and the state police informer shares in the unbelievable profits with the ever-loveable state cops.

Have you figured the return on a ten thousand dollar advance if it triples even once a week? You spend ten thousand dollars and it returns thirty thousand dollars. You spend thirty thousand dollars and it returns ninety thousand dollars. Ninety thousand dollars returns two hundred seventy thousand dollars. If you keep investing, the next return will put you over eight million dollars, if you haven't dipped into it or split it with cops and judges.
The eighth turnover could make your son ambassador to some

European country, and your grandson president of the U.S. of A. But the grandsons tend to begin listening to their own speechwriters and then Dallas happens. If you carry this drug investment to its conclusion, you pass twenty million dollars before you pass the eighth week and that buys one hell of a lot of respect and insulation. Or a pretty good political office. You beginning to get the picture?

The state cops can get maybe fifteen or twenty thousand dollars for a sting operation. This coal company is losing maybe fifty thousand dollars a day in idle equipment and unexploitables. Anyway, the coal companies, or CoCos, as we liked to refer to them, represented a huge investment in equipment and bribe money. Most of the coal was stolen one way or another during the reconstruction anyways. So if you think Kentucky was a Union State, go over to Frankfort and tour the Yankee barracks there. Bayonets have always had a sort of coercive effect on legislators, unless carried by the legislator's own troops, better known as state troopers.

There's this big investment producing nothing but rust, with its management staff sitting around waiting to see who gets fired or screwed next. Not necessarily in that order but you get the idea. Then, there's the transporting department, with maybe eight or ten multi-million dollar birds sitting around waiting to see which one will be scrapped or surplused next. Now I know it seems like I am running on too long with this, but try to bear with me and hear me out. This is necessary to set the stage for the rest of my story.

 OK, well, selling you equipment is like eating your seed potatoes. Once gone, you don't have a very good prospect of getting back into production. Even the Mafia was finally forced to go into the drug business, though over strong protests of the old-time dons. I got this information firsthand. Ever hear the name Guininc? The money was just irresistible. Simple economics.

The small demand that the state cops had been supplying for a generation or so suddenly exploded in the '60s and '70s into the biggest profit-maker since the British army forced the Chinese government to buy opium. When the price of oil suddenly caught up with the level of prices of everything else that had taken thirty years to reach, the sheiks gave a nod and Washington suddenly discovered that coal polluted the atmosphere with fly ash, sulfuric acid and all kinds of nasty shit.

Gasoline, of course, substitutes carbon monoxide for fly ash. Monoxide isn't really as objectionable because it's invisible, and who believes in what he can't see, right? Unless he happens to breathe too much of it. Then it doesn't matter what he believes.

Anyway, there are suddenly these vast tracts of ruined land that the coal companies are required by law to restore to their original contours. That's something like restoring the maidenhead of an ex-virgin — very difficult to do. So the company decides to use its wastelands, a vast and natural buffer zone, as a center for processing the hottest product in today's market. No, ha ha, I don't mean sex, that's number two. The drug user tends to lose interest in this commodity.

The investment is minimal. Some forms of the stuff are so addictive that the free samples the dealer passes out may well return ten thousand to a hundred thousand percent on the original investment, once the bait is taken and the hook is set. This is before the user's nose rots through from nostril to nostril, leaving him with a single blow hole, like a dolphin, only in his face instead of on the top of his head.

This is assuming he doesn't suffer incarceration after he has bungled a robbery or prostitution attempt, or interment if one of his victims turns out to be better armed than he — and with a steadier gun hand.

Now you may think I'm coming down too hard on the Kentucky State Police. I don't mean to. A lot of them (I'll go so far as to say most) are hard-working, honest shock troops in the somewhat ritualized war on crime. Maybe as many as seventy or seventy-five percent (yeah, most). Pretty much like in any other state force. I have personally known state troopers who were honest, hard-working people. It is truly unfortunate that they must bear the sins of their rat-assed brothers in blue.

"You have to keep things in perspective," Sean would say. "There are four branches of organized crime, and only four. The number of families doesn't matter a monkey's ass full of shit. All the branches complement each other like the corners of a square."

He'd usually pause here to roll a stick of Juicy Fruit into his mouth and grin at me. "The bottom corner on the right is the Mafia, on the right because they're so conservative, and business is on the left because they'll go in any direction where there's profit. Kind of like an old hound dog sniffing a bitch's ass. If it smells good, jump it.

"Now, what does that leave in the other two corners? Well might you ask, lad, might you ask." He'd sometimes sketch a square on a paper napkin and label the two lower corners.

"For their children? My, my, don't we hear that a lot these days. If they quit the Mob, some of them go into the church, so we have:

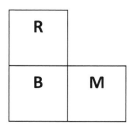

" ... Giving us religion for the third corner of the square. But the really ambitious ones urge their offspring into the ultimate racket. And do you know what that is, me boy?" Sean also liked to out-Irish the Irish character actors. "Why, bless you, me lad, it's only politics. Study on it.

"Read up on how the Mafia and the U.S. Army worked together on the invasion of the Italian Islands. Of course, that's an extreme and blatant example, easily overlooked in the press of war. The sailors on the Arizona and a lot of other ships are overlooked when the U.S. is blamed for nuking the poor, murdering Japs. Anyway, the U.S. Army proceeded to free all the Mafia soldiers old Benito Mussolini had canned away. Curious coincidence, no?"

Another time Sean had explained to me that if you "incinerate three hundred thousand Germans in a firestorm, like in Dresden, that's all right, so long as they're Caucasian and you use conceptual bombs to start the fires. If they're little brown men though, with slanted eyes that have been killing your brothers and uncles for years and you vaporize eighty thousand at once with a new weapon, that smacks of racism. Not to be mentioned, of course. You jump on the horror of it. What really bugs you is the efficiency.

"Eighty thousand human beings vaporized. Makes no difference if they were eighty thousand pieces of shit who would have bayoneted you in the back like they did the men who surrendered at Singapore, and raped the nurses as a matter of course. Once the pricks are gone, they become holy.

"How the shit did I wander so far from where I started? Back to the square. Ever hear of the Square of Opposition in logic? Look it up when you learn to read. The four corners of the square are: Mafia, Business, Religion, and Politics. Like your traditional triangle A B C, the square of society is M B R P, with all the vast wasteland in the middle reserved for all us nonentities who meet and meld our interests, flux, reflux, and pride ourselves on our honesty and honor and honorable intent. In other words, we pride ourselves on how well we've been suckered.

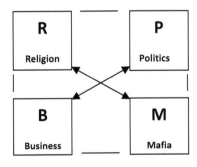

"Ever hear the expression 'God'll get you for that?' Of course you have. We all have. It's our rationale for letting someone get away with something we ought to stomp the living shit out of him for. And that, me lad, is where Old Mother Church enters into her corner of the square. All churches teach pretty much the same thing — you sin, you're punished — you do good works, you get your reward in heaven. Take your pleasure while you are alive and you'll either suffer eternal damnation, or your conscience will punish you so much you'll flog yourself into heaven.

"Reach back, lad, to your own Irish, Celtic and Nordic roots! Hel was the goddess of the dead who didn't die in battle. Not for me, lad. Not for me. Valhalla for me. Valhalla is reserved for those who die in battle. Did you ever wonder who was deader? Those who die in battle, or those who die in bed? Some say it was called the straw death — dying in bed. Today we'd scorn it as a Serta death or a waterbed death."

I shook my head. Bits of brain matter were drying on my arms and in my hair. I felt no guilt, just a mild inconvenience at the scraps of the dead that clung to me. I had rid the world of a foul thing. I knew I would have eaten dung to do it again to the same piece of shit. Sean had once sketched a short sword on a bar countertop with a beer-wet finger, then examined the crosspiece hand guard.

"That's powerful magic," Sean had said. "Taking an instrument of execution and converting it into a symbol of immortality. Powerful magic. Did you know that a Spanish priest with the conquistadors carried cruciform swords? Shaped like a cross. Powerful magic. The theory was that any Indians killed with such a sword would instantly be converted to the one true faith, hence going to heaven and receiving a harp. "Ah, the evil men do!" He fell silent for a time, grinning slightly at his private thoughts. Then he went on:

"Do you remember the time you were up on wanton endangerment charges?" I knew then that he had been researching me. I had simply gotten to my single-six faster than the man trespassing on the coal company's land could get to his shotgun. He shouldn't have had it hanging in the rack of his pickup's rear window. I wouldn't let him off the road to turn around, so he had to back up nearly a mile. Even at thirteen I knew he couldn't risk trying to score with a twelve-gauge while backing up.

He turned out to be a sore loser and swore out the complaint (I never did like the Johnsons). The coal company lawyer defended me and the charge was finally dismissed after years of hanging in limbo and after the original charge had been bumped up to attempted murder. A few years later, when the coal boom was over and the coke boom had taken place, and all the new highways were finished, he'd have simply disappeared into one of the countless old auger holes along the road. Maybe he did.

"You probably thought that right had triumphed, now didn't you? Your father was hired to guard the property, so you had the right to help him out."

I waited. That was exactly what I had assumed.

"Well, what became of your attorney?"

"He ran for Commonwealth Attorney, after the mines began shutting
down."

"Of course he did. And it wasn't just a spur of the moment decision. He now decides, by the way, what warrants will be issued in three counties. You see, under Kentucky law a victim does not have the right to a warrant. No, no, and hell's no! That might lead to bothersome complaints against prominent citizens — campaign contributors, for example. And elected officials!

"Now if the complaint is against an outsider, and remember, my boy, you are an outsider, or a non-voter, the warrant and the fines generally follow quickly enough. Especially if the plaintiff is local and can garner a few votes, or spare a few dollars for campaign expenses, of course. Oh, yes, don't forget about some of the fastest trials in the country. And your family, on your mother's side, represented a big block of votes. I hate to destroy an illusion, but it was bad political business to bring you to trial, so it wasn't done. So much for integrity in the courts.

"Integrity in the courts, now there's a scary fucking thought!"
Sean talked on, though my mind was beginning to wander. As always, when coming off the high of a date, I began to get as horny

as if I were on a real date. No shrink ever tried to explain to me the symbolism in shooting lead into someone and then getting the urge to shoot semen into someone else. I don't know if it was envy of the power of the load I was shooting, or the urge to symbolically recreate life. Either way it was fun. For both of us, I hoped.

However, my wife had noticed the connection between my absences and my sex drive. I believe any other woman would have been flattered and assumed it was because I had missed her.

Not Frieda. Not that bitch. Her response after the first raid had been, "What happened? Some whore get you worked up when she was on the rag?" Rag? Hell, *she* was always on the rag. After her comments, you can imagine how long it took me to go from flagstaff to laggard. After one of her "out with a whore" comments once, I shot back, "Now honey, you know I wasn't out with no whore — you were home."

And it wasn't as if she hadn't known, or at least guessed what I was doing. She really didn't care, as long as I brought home my thousand a week in untaxed cash. And believe you me, a thousand bucks did not go far with her. There was nothing illegal about my unreported income. The groups did not exist, therefore our paymaster, Richards, could not hand the members a thousand dollars each week we were on call. Sean always said that was a Jesuitical way of looking at the situation. The group did not exist; therefore, it had no paymaster to issue cash to group members who did not exist. If neither group nor paymaster existed, no money could change hands. When I asked him if we did not then fail to exist, along with the money, he merely grinned and said, "Naturally."

But right then, I existed. The drying brain matter in my hair was starting to prickle despite my efforts to concentrate on the upcoming debriefing. I was thinking of all the pairs of smooth thighs I had ever crawled between, or bent over a desktop in high school. I wanted the taste of salty sweet breast in my mouth and the feel of long hair in my face. Even the wildcat raking and biting of a scratcher would have been welcome as the Cherokee chassis swayed into and out of holes in what passed as a road.

Eastern Kentucky is Republican, and the old pork barrel had been dry from 1932 to present. Even Mr. toll-road Bert Combs hadn't bothered to penetrate Martin County. After all, the only way you could go east from there was into West Virginia, another state entirely.

Sean had once pointed out the irony of West Virginia's existence. At the time when old Longshanks (most know him as Abe Lincoln) was expending scores of thousands of lives to prove that secession of states was not legal, he gladly accepted secession of part of a state from the whole. And the only other organizations I ever heard of that you can't get out of are the British Empire, in the case of Northern Ireland, and the Mafia.

The Cherokee hit a narrow blacktop road and sped up as Sean's drone continued. Across from me, one of the other Unicorns was looking bored. In the front seat, one head was nodding drowsily. Two of the three faces were new to me. I wondered if they were permanent replacements or odd-job workers —independent contractors from the borderland. Maybe low-rank Mafia taking on a special job. I decided that it wasn't likely, and really didn't matter.

In our circle, it's a standing joke that the only difference between working for the Mafia and working for the government is that the Mafia pays better. The rocking of the Jeep chassis lulled me and pretty soon, I was thinking of Nancy. One of only two good things to come out of this whole damned affair. She was a good woman, but she made a mistake, a big mistake, she cared for me. Nancy. She had brought me down before from my killing high.

Always there was the fierce quick coupling. A grasping as if for something permanent and lasting. A pouring out and pouring into each other of all we held back of ourselves. All that we reserved to ourselves from Jack Hillard of the Kentucky state police, Richards — whoever he worked for — and the DEA.

My mind was going to be on her during the debriefing, not that anyone would notice. If I dragged a little in answering, it would be put down to fatigue, except maybe by some analyst who spent his days in some soundproof cubicle listening to the tapes of the debriefing.

We came out of the debriefing as a muggy dawn was fingering the hills over toward West Virginia. Warm for early autumn. Not as warm as I was. My little Dodge Colt ticked right over. I had previously owned a Scout, but Richards had suggested I get rid of it — too suggestive of rugged types of outdoor activity. You know, too much of a 'man' thing.

Anyway, the Colt purred right along for the forty-two miles I needed to get to Nancy's apartment. I parked two blocks away and walked to the apartment, which was over the drug store. In these little mountain towns, you don't park near your girl's house. I once knew a teacher who lost his job because he loaned his car to his girl and it was seen parked in her driveway all night. No one ever said Sheldon Clark High School hired intelligent people. The tension was getting to me as the first cars began to move over the deserted streets. I used my key to let myself into Nancy's apartment.

CHAPTER 3

Now, don't get the idea that I'm going to give you a step-by-step replay of my lovemaking. Nor are you going to get any essays on my philosophy of sex. If you need the replay, you are either a beginner or a voyeur. I think that's kind of perverted, I mean. As for the second, sex isn't a philosophy; it's an urge, and a primal one at that.

And speaking of perverts and voyeurs, Inez is full of them. Just ask around. Some are even hired as school principals. Anyway, you have got to be wondering by now just what this little group I am calling the Unicorns is, and who was bossing us and who was paying us. You know, several of us came to wonder the same thing.

Back in the little Appalachian town where I grew up, a few people got more than their share of respect. One was a doctor who had to be a smart man. Another was the school superintendent who was in a position of major power. I remember hearing of one over in Breathitt County who was admired greatly. Her name was Jackie B. Smith, and her husband was county judge. You'd be surprised at the things that become legal when you are married to the man who has the last word about what is legal in your county. The laws have changed some since then and whole new sets of thieves have come into their own, but Jackie B. and Ivan Smith are well remembered. There this old country saying, "You've got to do with what you've got to do with."

[Look, I know this stuff is boring, but it's important you understand the minds from this area. Sorry, please read on.]

Now, Jackie B. had a job as school superintendent, and that

meant she controlled three or four hundred jobs. That means a lot of votes when you count spouses and relatives, and mountain folks are clannish. It is sort of like hire one/buy all. Anyway, with her husband running the county, Jackie B. instated her own anti-poverty program, long before L.B.J. did. It was simple. A sort of reversal or modification on the Marxism principle. Her reasoning was from each, according to his ability, to me, according to my wants. This sounds just about like the other small town Marxists, sorry, I meant to say county officials. Ah, what the hell. Marxists.

The application of her plan was simple: She just charged each public school student in Breathitt County a dollar a month to ride the public school buses. Now that's simple, and ingenious. You collect the money and the public picks up the tab for buses, drivers and maintenance. Of course, you choose who is paid for maintenance, but that's gravy and votes. A dollar a month doesn't sound like much does it? But there were nine thousand kids enrolled in the Breathitt County schools, and the schools were open nine months a year.

County judges actually held court in those days, and parents could be fined five bucks a day for letting their kids miss school. Never mind most of these so-called county judges couldn't read or write their own name (Inez has a few of those), the power was theirs just the same. So, with twenty school days a month, a dollar a month was a bargain. Jackie B. was so admired in Kentucky that the Democratic Party made her its state chairwoman. Who said the Democrats didn't know a good thief/family member when they saw one? Although I must say, I doubt it would have made a difference if she had been a Republican. All shit runs downhill and stinks just the same.

Anyway, I don't know *really* what she did with that measly little dollar a month, times nine a year, times nine thousand kids, but I do know after twenty years or so, old Ivan opened up a brand new bank in Jackson, the county seat. But I digress (I know, I digress a lot. Sorry). I started to tell you how I got into this sideline, and who was footing the bill.

My first contact with the group named the Unicorns came

through one of the most awesomely respected professionals of the Kentucky State Police. My father had gotten pretty well stoved up in his career of contracting and lumbering timber. He was still strong as a bull, but his endurance was gone. Oh, he could still outlast any two men in a physical confrontation, but his days of wrestling twenty-foot logs onto forty-foot trailers were over.

About that time, the job of town marshal fell open, for one reason or another. The old marshal had either died or retired on his kickback money. There are three ways to get a political job in Kentucky:

1. Know somebody;
2. Know something on somebody;
3. Be kind to a lot of people who know how the levers in a voting machine work.

As I said, the job fell empty and my father was offered the position. You know the kind of job I mean. The kind where local teenagers make a game of stealing your 'slapstick' (user-friendly jargon for blackjack) out of your pocket while you're on patrol. I think it paid something like eight hundred dollars a month. I have since come to suspect that the town fathers expected it to be augmented by whatever amount the marshal chose to shake down the local bootleggers, whores, and petty thieves for.

Only one thing. Dad was too honest for his own good. So when he actually started making arrests, the town fathers had a shit hemorrhage. But more about that in my next book. At any rate, my father became town marshal.

By this time, I had been doing a man's work in logging camps, and had come to a man's strength by the time I was fourteen. A stray karate enthusiast from Morehead State University had gotten me into the sport, and I wound up being the first black belt in the county. You think that sounds good? Here was an unpopular kid who was muscle-bound from man-killing work and who was supposed to be some kind of expert like Kung Fu on the tube. Now, those old boys from Eastern Kentucky can teach the Missourians a thing or two when it comes to "show me!"

By the time I finished my sophomore year of high school, I had fought with every redneck jackwagon on campus, usually in pairs after the first few fights. I learned quickly there is no substitute for being determined to win. I left behind me a trail of broken noses, broken jaws, dislocated hips and shoulders and crushed nuts.

You know, it never seemed to matter if I was jumped by a half-dozen guys in the smoking area at good old Sheldon Clark High; it was always "Duncan's fault." I was damned if I did, and damned if I didn't. No wonder I am the way that I am.

I grew up pretty much a loner. My brothers went in for basketball and baseball and took out their anger by bashing other bodies in a ruled and regulated situation. They never became high school heroes, but they did release a lot of frustration and rage.

I didn't. I took it to heart. It became my life blood; embalmed and treasured up to a life beyond life, but of deeds beyond those believed in by the average dumbass citizen who thinks this country or any country runs by written law. What a country runs on his power. And I learned to use the power that physical strength represented. One of my regrets about the lifestyle I developed was the effect it had on my mother. I must have driven her half out of her mind.

While my brothers and sister were begging to try helping her around the house, I was pursuing my own lifestyle, and pursuing it alone in the rugged hill country of Eastern Kentucky. Now, don't get me wrong, I did more than my share of work on the family farm. I just didn't do what I considered to be wimpy work. If it was hard, I did it. If it was heavy, I loved it. But when the work was done, I was in the mountains. I could tell you where every old still in the county was located. I had watched moonshiners run off enough illegal shine to float the kind of coast guard cutter Jack Kennedy's granddad used to dodge when he was founding the family fortune.

Of course, in my county everybody drank 'shine and a lot of them made it. Back in those days the treasury agents — your classic revenuers — still took an occasional interest in such activities. A little later, I got pissed at one moonshiner because he took a shot at me. I didn't mind the shot. What pissed me off was that he holed my backpack. Anyway, I learned how the system works when I reported him to the revenuers. They told me to call the state police. When I told them I had been watching a K.S.P. car being loaded with hooch for delivery, they told me it must have been confiscated and hung up. I waited a month till I knew the shooter was off in Lexington buying corn and sugar. I took my little hatchet and chomped his worm into two-foot sections and I plugged the outlet.

Well, to make a long story short, I rigged this bastard moonshiner's still to blow. I missed seeing the explosion. But I sure as hell didn't miss feeling it. I'd been aiming at the crest of a ridge when I found myself lifted up and tumbled into the scrub of second growth pines ahead of me. When I stood up, the still site looked like the mouth of a volcano. Only it wasn't lava that was pouring out and falling on me. It was shredded copper. It was a lovely sight, and my little hatchet was still clasped in my hand. I gathered up my backpack and made fast time toward another part of the county. There was going to be a very unhappy moonshiner at the head of this hollow in a day or two, and I was careful not to leave any tracks or traces.

But damn, I hated to waste all that shine. But the bastard had it coming!

I knew he hadn't really seen me when he'd taken that shot at me, and I guess I should have been grateful to him. He taught me that people engaged in illegal activities tend to be murderous, even though they're working for those who are supposed to be upholding the law. I got leery of all law officers for a long time, and this wariness spread to the politicians directing the law enforcement.

Later, the sheriff posted a reward for information leading to the arrest and conviction of the person who set fire to a barn on the moonshiner's place. The Baptist preacher delivered a sermon on the evils of theft, arson, and hiding your sins, because you can't hide them from the all-seeing God. I'm sure the Baptist preacher missed his nip along with a lot of other high profile county members. To compound my sin, I told my mother I tore my clothes when a fallen pine trunk broke under me as I was crossing a shallow ravine. After my experience with the revenuers, my claim seemed as reasonable as the one that says, "All men are created equal."

But as I had learned at school, equality didn't necessarily coincide with fairness, and by the middle of my junior year, I had left school. It wasn't academics, it was simply a matter of quitting or being expelled for winning too many fights I had never started in the first damned place or my parents being sued over their idiot son. The best I can figure it, if you won a fight you must have started it, even if the other side had you outweighed by thirty pounds or outnumbered two or three to one. That placed me on my own, and my father in the marshal's office.

I found ways of getting out of the hills. Fighting as a kickboxer semipro was one way. Dad had started coaching me when I was nine. But the hills had a way of calling me back (I wish I had turned the volume off to *that* song). This was home, and if I could find a way of using what I knew to make a living, I was determined to try.

I opened my first karate school in Paintsville, Kentucky, much to the distaste of the Shaolin boys. I had the most eager bunch of incompetents I never hope to see again. But they learned well. There is a mean streak in native Kentuckians that loves to exploit anything that seems like dirty fighting. That is, they love to win almost as much as I do. But there weren't enough customers in one town to make the kind of living I wanted.

By this time, I had three schools in three different towns. My hometown had become sophisticated enough to want a police chief instead of a town marshal, so my father was elevated to that position. Sometime before that, when I was still a kid, a new state cop had been assigned to our area. He was lean but with a slight tendency to chubbiness. I remember when he first came in to introduce himself to my father.

"I'm your new state trooper," he said, in a tone that might have meant 'I'm you're new bishop or archdeacon.' "My name is Hillard. Jack Hillard." And he laughed, that easy big-man's laugh I was to know for years. Years later, though, I would come to hate that laugh almost as much as I grew to hate the man. Jack Hillard. Friend, mentor, role model, recruiter, bastard and lying back-stabbing son of a bitch. I am fully aware of the significance the mountaineers attach to the last term; men have died for using it. The reason runs thusly: a man is a son of a bitch; therefore, his mother is a bitch. Call a man's mother a bitch and you invite grave consequences. Pun intended. I'll take the dare! Nobody got to be such an all around bastard prick cocksucker in one generation, with the possible circumstance that the bastards could have been on his father's side.

From the time Jack Hillard entered our lives, he was always around, gushing over the way my father acted as a quieting influence on Inez and Martin County. The county sheriff was theoretically the power in the county, of course, but then there was much that centered in Inez, hence in my father's jurisdiction.

It never occurred to me in those days — remember, I was only a kid at the time — that there was anything unusual in a state trooper flattering my father. I have since learned that a county law enforcement officer can be pretty susceptible when the state boys move in and begin uttering compliments. Of course, that wouldn't be a problem if all the state police were honest. As I said, Jack Hillard was a bastard of the first water, and the water was filled with shit.

Inez was too small to support a donut shop, so Jack Hillard was usually to be found hanging around the local Colonel Sanders. I remember thinking once that it was odd he was always sucking on a drumstick or the butt of a wing. A little later, I realized that he was always served by a redheaded waitress who wore her blouse too tight and nothing under it, her cleavage squeezed together in a tight vee. Once from the outside of the restaurant, I saw her shrug a nipple out of her top and quickly palm it back inside.

Later, I learned that she had a brother in La Grange prison who was coming up for parole. I didn't think too much of that, till I found out that Jack was the arresting officer. The judge had recommended parole. I don't know whether the brother was guilty of whatever he was charged with or not, but he got paroled. Kentucky is quite as advanced as New York or Chicago in convicting someone in order to bring pressure on a third someone. But I digress, again. Hey, I'm sorry, okay!

Jack Hillard was our new state trooper. He flattered my father for his enforcement of the law. He flattered my progress as a fighter. He supported my advancements in karate. He knocked up the waitress at the Colonel Sanders and her brother got paroled. Jack Hillard was a bastard and a son of a bitch, but he represented Kentucky's finest. Does that give you any cause to pause and reflect? It makes me want to puke.

As I said, he was a bastard and a backstabbing son of a bitch. But he grew on you. Kind of like a fungus, or a hemorrhoid. He was of above average height, well over the six-foot mark. He tended to be pudgy, or would after he'd hung around the Colonel Sanders for a few years. His face tended to be round. Brach cephalic was the way Sean later described him. It was easy to picture him with a Charlie Brown type head. If he hadn't been a state trooper you might never have noticed him, or else taken him as a pimp for one of the lower-class whores. I wouldn't be surprised if he had invited my father to join the Lyon's Club.

Glenda Lyons was the whore who worked a four or five county circuit, and among the teenage boys in the area, the Lyons Club was the joking euphemism for screwing Glenda Lyons. It had one thing in common with the other clubs; you had to pay to be a member, or to use your attached member.

He was a state pooper. I mean trooper, and, like many an asshole in uniform, was respected (and feared) because he wore the uniform. But always he was a shade too friendly, a touch too hearty in his questions. He embarrassed me by being — though I didn't know the word at the time — too obsequious. In short, he was lacking in reserve. I didn't know at the time that he tended to lose himself in his work. He wasn't real. He became this manufactured personality. I realized later he probably would have made an excellent Boy Scout troop leader for the younger boys. I was sixteen by this time, and in many ways unsophisticated enough to accept the appearance he projected, to my uneasiness. After all, I was just a kid, and he was state police.

Let me explain the hierarchy of Kentucky. The sheriff cannot succeed himself (I understand that's been changed now). In theory, this is to prevent his becoming too well entrenched. Actually, it's only an inconvenience. There are counties where sheriff and chief deputy positions are exchanged back and forth by the two same men for decades.

More permanent was the county judge, who could succeed himself. This was a real judgeship before a new law reduced the position to the equivalent of county mayor. A freelance truck driver, for example, might meet practically all the voters in the county over the course of twenty or thirty years. Or, he could work at the gas company. Then at retirement, he'd be well enough known to run for county judge with a good chance of winning. Having been in business, he'd been careful not to offend anyone, specially the heads of the old-time moonshining and pot-growing clans. Lots of votes back up in those hollows.

Anyway, he might not be able to read the donor card on the back of his driver's license, but he could be a judge until too feeble to make up laws. Don't get me wrong, some of those old boys had a better idea of what law was for than most. But, alas, the system is gone now. The overpopulation of lawyers realized that here were prize plums in the basket and rewrote the book to give the renamed county judge executive only part of his old power.

CHAPTER 4

Author's Note:
This chapter has nothing to do with my work with the Unicorns.
It is to briefly show you, the reader, the type of environment I grew
up in. That violence will always be part of my life. Hey, I make no
apologies; it made me tough and taught me that I could endure.
Hell, I even learned to enjoy it a little. Remember, I was only sixteen
years old at this time.

It was a week after Dad became marshal that the Spyders, West Virginia's self-proclaimed "bad-ass motorcycle punks" showed themselves in Inez, and it was late one August afternoon when they rode into town. They came in on Route 40, straight out of the ass state. We figured they had high-tailed it out of the state for a cooling-off period. Like the city boys they basically were, they figured by the time they came back, tempers would have cooled and things would be done by the law, if anything was done at all. After all, one scared sixty-six year old fart wasn't going to do much against twenty-two men in what passed as their prime.

What they did not reckon on was that they were not in the big city now, and if Sid had enough sense to be scared of them, they would not have had to stove in his ribs and break his nose in the first place. Anyway, Sid's ratty old van brought word that the Spyders were mustering at the Turkey Creek churchyard (ironic, wasn't it?).

He had gotten close enough to see them, rolling grass and swilling Jim Beam. I found out later he had used a pair of ten by fifty Jason binoculars. When the sound of the bike motors reached us, Dad strolled across to the corner of Middlefork Road and Main, where he leaned against a telephone pole, whittling long strips of bark from a green hickory stick about the size of a baseball bat on its big end. He had a Winchester 12-gauge pump tucked under the arm that held the stick, and the knife he was using was a foot-long switchblade.

I knew that the whittling was all an act — a hayseed or Fetchet act. You leave the victim with a sense of superiority, and then spring the trap. Anyway, the Spyders throttled down and came into town at not much more speed than a high noon walk. I will never forget the look on those thirty or so faces, some of which had what seemed to be the female gender of some nearly related species riding pillion (but I do admit, it was hard to tell the difference between the sexes of this group). It was the look you get from those who think they are lords of the earth, but who are really, in all actuality, just puffed up pieces of shit.

Dad grinned. "Bluff," he said, and waved me aside. I knew what we were dealing with. When they stopped about twenty feet from my dad, I could see images on their colors. A purple Italian sports car mounted by a black widow spider. Only the spider was anatomically incorrect, as I suspected more than one of the Spyders were, too.

The leader called himself John Paul Jones and looked like he had been assembled by the wardrobe department of a cheap biker movie. He had it all down, the jacket with the sleeves hacked off, replica iron cross on the chest, replica swastikas on his pocket, replica dagger at his side. Only the heavy chain he wore as a belt was authentic. I have since come to think of him having a replica brain of one of the midrange primates (no offense to primates intended). He chewed a cigar and amber ran into his whiskers from the corner of his mouth. He didn't have a beard, he just hadn't shaved for a week or ten days. "Hungry, studs?" he called over the rumble of twenty-two idling engines. "Looks like the town done got itself a marshal, just like in the Wild West! Dinner is served."

Dad stepped into the street to a chorus of "Screw him," and "Fuck the law," and "Kill the fucker."

"Mister Jones," Dad said mildly, and I began to get scared. When a mountain man is quiet, he is the most dangerous. "I believe there is a warrant for your arrest on assault and battery charges over at the sheriff's office."

"So what, shitface?" Jones rolled his cigar and spat. "Even if I did slap the old fart around, he asked for it. Wouldn't sell to us 'cause he said he was closed. We got rights, too. Besides, I got twenty-one witnesses that say I was at a drinking and screwing party over in Mingo County that afternoon, clean out of the fucking state." His gang nodded.

"Your whole club?" Dad asked.

"Fuckin' right." Jones nodded.

"Just twenty-one witnesses," Dad nodded, and Jones's cigar stopped. He saw where this was headed and was beginning to boil. "Don't you fellows ever invite any girls to your screwing parties?" Dad asked. There was a giggle from one of the females on the bikes, cut off by the sound of a slap.

"I believe we can discuss this situation." Dad stepped forward. As he did so, his right arm arched up and the front inch of the switchblade was buried in the tough creosote wood of the telephone pole at his back.

Jones swung off his bike and stepped forward. "We got nothing to discuss, fuzzy balls." His gang began to dismount as Jones dropped his hand to hook his thumb in a ring on his belt. I knew that a pull on that ring would free the three or four feet of heavy chain.

"I could welcome you to the valley," Dad offered, and shifted his hickory club to his right hand as he took a step forward. Then he turned his back as he did so, and I saw Jones pull the ring on his belt. He and Dad had moved within six feet of each other when Dad turned his back on him. My eyes were on Jones as his eyes followed the club. Instead of swinging it at him, Dad merely lowered it, and then flipped it back toward the telephone pole.

I never saw what happened then. I was trying to watch the white stick turning in the air when the blue steel chain dropped free in Jones's hand. One thing I am sure of, a twelve gauge Magnum pump with seven rounds aboard is heavier than two feet of half carved hickory, and its oiled walnut stock is harder with sharper edges. Whatever the movement Dad had to go through, the first thing I knew, he had the Winchester gripped in both hands and had slammed the steel butt plate into Jones' face.

As Jones' chain clinked into a pile on the asphalt, I heard Dad say warmly, "Welcome to the valley." Then all hell broke loose. There were still twenty-one men on their feet and they were scrambling for weapons. I saw chains, knives, daggers, tools, revolvers and so help me a couple of Lugers and other assorted automatics.

I think that day I began to understand the physiology of the biker. With twenty-one frenzied armed men and a few women charging him, Dad calmly raised the shotgun and blew the cylinder head off a Goldwing. The six thousand dollar bike hiccupped and died. While the mob stared at the smoking Honda, Dad worked the slide on his pump and took aim at a Kawasaki gas tank, and the bikers were scrambling to save their property.

Dad stood there, calmly working the slide of that shotgun. In school, I had read a line by Poe that said, "At every word a reputation died." Now I knew what it meant. Rifle slugs for a twelve gauge weigh five hundred grams, are about the size of a small man's thumb, and cost about forty-five cents apiece (at least they did then). In less than ten seconds, I saw a little more than three dollars worth of ammunition destroy thirty thousand dollars worth of machinery — with help from the ruptured gas tanks. Dad went for the more expensive bikes even in the heat of battle.

But a Winchester pump holds only seven rounds. Normally, these are double-ought buck shells, but when you're huntin' motorcycle, you need the extra punch of that big chunk of solid lead. Whatever round you use, you have to reload, and that few seconds gives the opposition time to regroup. That's exactly what happened to Dad.

He slid the empty magazine tube out of the Winchester. It rang hollowly as it hit the asphalt. The gang was on him as he reached behind him for the second magazine he carried in a holder at his shoulder. As he had fired he had been backing up, and was now at the telephone pole. I saw the magazine torn from his hand after he jammed it into the throat of the first biker to reach him. I knew what he was thinking: the odds were about right.

The reaching hand came down and something flashed silver. Just once, though. Then the stiletto blade was the color of the butcher knives my grandfather used on hogs each November. One man's reaching hand was suddenly white above a gushing wrist. The red blade flickered and a throat gushed bright. On the follow-through, the hand turned and I heard the brittle snap of a collarbone, the fourth man's belt was sliced open and he was all but disemboweled. Then something hit the pole behind Dad's shoulder. It seemed seconds before I recognized the sound of a shot. One of the greasebags was standing on top of a pair of shot-up bikes and shooting over the heads of the mob with a rusty-looking Walther.

In the split second of silence after the shot I heard, "Now shit, boys." Then the Walther was spinning away from the arm that held it, away from the arm and part of the hand. The other part was still tangled in the trigger guard when the mangled pistol landed twenty feet from its screaming owner. Twenty yards up the street a haze of blue-gray smoke drifted out the rusty window frame of Sid's van.

I guess Sid was busy right then, reloading one barrel of his old ten gauge double. Some of the juice leaked out of those fingers as the Walther flew over the heads of the gang and seemed to have a calming effect on them. When they stirred, I realized Sid wasn't reloading. He had been catching his breath. A ten gauge punches a wallop in both directions, and Sid was frail. Anyway, his second barrel took the ass half off another would-be Wyatt Earp.

By this time, Dad had recovered both the Winchester and the magazine. I had not fired a shot from the Marlin 30–30 I was holding. But now I stepped out and leveled a round into the chamber. I hadn't seen so much blood since the hog killings I mentioned before.

"Halt!" My father's voice called through the clink of chains and the moans of causalities. "Get the fuck out of my town." To a man, they halted. "Take the garbage with you," he told them. "Leave the trash." They looked at him for a moment, and then went off to Sid's van. That little blue-gray cloud was there again, of course.

A single revolver started to rise, but two shotguns and my rifle finally registered on whatever was left of the biker's brain, and the steel thunked to the pavement. The sound was followed by the rattle of knives and the clink of chains.

"You!" Dad pointed to a husky biker with the side of his head shaved. "Which bike is yours?"

"The Hog." Shaved head pointed to one of the undamaged cycles.

"Get his hand, put him on it and get him the hell out of here. The rest of the bikes stay. Roll!"

Shaved Head looked like he didn't want to touch that shot-damaged Walther, even to retrieve the piece of hand that was still tangled in the trigger guard. If there is such a thing as a collective shudder, I think I saw it there. The tough guys must have looked pretty much the same as the punks at Kent State had looked when they found out violence can be met with violence. They never rolled, but by the time Shaved Head was out of sight, they certainly slunk. But before they had gone, Dad walked up to Jones, who was sitting up. I saw him reach for the length of chain he had dropped when Dad clobbered him.

"Welcome to the valley." Dad set one foot on the end of the chain and I noticed he was wearing the steel-toed engineered boots he had favored when wrestling oak and pine logs out of the hollow. He deliberately drew back his right foot and bent his left leg for more leverage. As the hard rubber heel broke Jones's jaw, nose, and left the flesh on the left side of his face hanging in one thick flap, he went on in the same mild voice, "And meet the meanest son of a bitch in the valley."

I had once stumbled and done a botched job of cutting the throat of an old barren sow Granddad was butchering. The knife slashed her throat some but plunged on into the front of her breast. She screamed horribly before Grandpa grabbed the knife and slit her throat properly. Jones' screams sounded just like the old sows.

As I grew into manhood, I would think back on that day. I felt no fear. I did not freeze. But I felt left out. It was during this event that I knew deep down in my soul that I could take the life of another man. Calmly, and with a smile. May the Gods have mercy on me, for I did it so many times as a Unicorn, it felt natural.

CHAPTER 5

By the time I was twenty, I had a beautiful daughter, an ex-wife and schools in three little mountain towns. Jack Hillard, too, was married and living in a half-million dollar house one of the coal barons had built and then decided to rent out because it wasn't good enough for his new wife. I envied Jack being able to afford it on a policeman's salary. Anyway, Hemorrhoid, I mean, Jack, had continued to stop in at one or the other of my schools whenever his schedule allowed.

On this particular Saturday, we were sitting around my Inez school, half-heartedly watching a football game on T.V. and splitting a twelve pack of Coors. Jack always drank Coors, and he would drive to West Virginia to get it if he hadn't come through any wet territory on the way home. I preferred Guinness, or mead. You know, a man's drink. But it was impossible to get it in this part of Kentucky. So I had to settle for stump water. Jack kept up a running commentary on the game, acting like a fat little coach we used to have at Sheldon Clark High back in the old days. Then he got quiet, as we finished our fourth beer. He rested his bottle on his knee and looked at me.

"Little buddy," he began, and I laughed, because he reminded me of Rosco P. Coletrane on "The Dukes of Hazzard." "Little buddy," he went on. "How'd you like to make some real money?"

"I don't know. Is it legal?" I asked him.

"Legal as you want to make it." He burped. "That's entirely up to you."

I looked at him through my bottle and one eye seemed magnified beyond normal.

"Look, little brother," he started again. "I know you hate dope as much as I do. Basically what you would be doing is joining a group that goes after drug dealers and the people who are behind them. You might never hit the one who actually got your brother hooked on the shit, but you certainly will hit others like him."

"Tell me more, man." I swilled my beer, thinking of the old Luger I had in my desk drawer and the sleek MAC-10 a dealer had let me fire once when he was trying to sell it to my Dad.

"A new squad is being put together right now." Jack unscrewed the cap from another Coors. "Its job will be to seek information about drug dealing by the big shots in the county and this state and other states and faraway places. Whenever and wherever they're brought to our attention."

I nodded. My mind began to shift into high gear.

"If they're just regular dealers, we'll arrest them and put them on trial. But you might as well know, some of these dealers are above the law. You'll have car dealers, lawyers, bankers, mining company executives, cops, you name it — they're involved. They are too respectable to be arrested, much less committed. It's a cruel fact of life, little buddy, but in this state — and I suspect pretty much the world over — the penalty suits the social or economic position of the criminal, in reverse ratio. Basically, the poor commit crimes, while the rich commit *indiscretions*. Those are the ones we want to go after. The big boys that are above the law."

"Count me in," I told him.

"There's only one thing," he went on as if I hadn't spoken. "You have to be twenty-one, and you're only twenty."

"Shit."

"Yeah, that means you have a couple of months to think about it. I'll level with you, it can get dangerous. But the pay is a thousand dollars a week in cash while you're on call. It's a service for your country as well as a chance to get back at the kind of people who ruined your brother. Think about it."

What twenty-year-old could resist the chance to get at the

throat of the kind of people he was talking about? And get paid a thousand bucks a week?

"Think about it." Jack knocked off the last of his beer. "If you're still interested in two months, you'll be contacted by our people. Your schools. You'll need to keep them operating both for the money and for the cover they'd provide you."

"Why would I need cover if I am on the law's side?" I asked him. "Seems like we'd just do it."

"We might just do it," he said, "But there is a whole vast bureaucracy out there called the IRS, and they frown on un taxable cash payments. And frankly, we suspect there may be some people in the Revenue Service who are supplementing their own salaries by selling information we'd rather not have given out."

It made sense, and I was willing to wait. Besides, I really would have to find suitable people to do what I'd been trying to handle on my own. I'd barely done this when my twenty-first birthday came up. I was still suffering from a post-birthday hangover, when a knock came at the door of my Inez school while I was trying to sleep it off. Here it was, ten o' clock in the evening and these two suit and tie gentlemen were knocking on my door and entering when I opened up. They presented credentials identifying them as Drug Enforcement Agency operators — DEA. The names, I noticed, were Smith and Jones. Oh no, I thought, another TV show.

"We understand you might be interested in serving your country," Smith or Jones said, and I stared at them. I couldn't tell them apart.

"I already did." I told him, through a mouth that was a little dry.

That didn't stop him. He went on to tell me what a great service I'd be in a position to do for my country, and my family, and my hometown. It was the same patriotic sucker drivel that had been spewed since Roman times and it even had a touch of J.F.K's "Ask Not" speech thrown in. Aside from that, it might have been made by Roosevelt's recruiters, or Napoleon's, or Bismarck's, or Hitler's. Only the words change to suit the language and the times.

"Okay, okay," I finally cut them off. "Shit, I'm in." Hell's bells, I was ready to stand up, take a crap and start singing the Star

Spangled Banner.

"Fine. You'll be contacted by Officer Hillard in the next week to ten days. You'll be taken to Lexington for the formal swearing-in, then later to Virginia for standard training and testing in weapons proficiency, and physiological suitability. Smith or Jones stood up and offered me his hand. "Welcome," he said, "to our side." The handshake was studiedly firm.

Then the matched pair of them strolled out into the night air and got into the nondescript gray Buick. Whoever was driving executed a tight U-turn and the car disappeared in the direction of West Virginia. I went back to enjoying my hangover and wondering how long I would have to wait to hear from Jack. The wait took five days.

The following Wednesday, he showed up at my Paintsville school and put on his sweats. After a little sparring, he followed me to the water fountain. As I bent over the pencil stream of water, he laughed and spoke in a conversational tone.

"Be ready to leave at five in the morning from the Inez school."

He then wandered on out and I heard his LTD drive away. Though he hadn't yet reached the grade of detective at this time, Jack had two cars he alternated between. One was the regular gray Crown Victoria with the strip and the blue bubble light on top. The second was your regulation white unmarked Crown Victoria with a small antenna rising from the upper edge of the trunk lid. There were times I would look at that car and think to myself, "pimp car." It was the second car, the pimp car, that picked me up as dawn was breaking the next morning.

Jack ran through the usual patter as the car rolled through Hazzard and headed for London. At London, he stopped long enough to get coffee and try to hit on a cute little red- headed waitress who seemed to know him. As we left he said, half angry and half regretful, "I've been working on that slut for two months and can't score. She's twenty-four and divorced. She must have somebody in the woodwork."

I said, "Maybe you're not her type," and he gave me a funny look.

"There's only two types, little brother," he told me. "Stickin' out and opened open. 'Male and female, He created them,' as the Book says. The goddamn world's black and white. Good and bad, cock and cunt, us and them. Keep it simple and go for the gusto. I'll serve her yet! I've got what she needs. And she's got what I want. It's just a matter of making her realize she wants it too."

At the time, I agreed with Jack. I thought he really liked the girl, and she didn't seem bothered by him. I began to wonder when he stopped in Richmond and swung by Eastern Kentucky University for a long chat with a short brunette who was carrying textbooks under her arm. Jack seemed to fare better here, for I heard him tell her he'd see her tonight.

"Got to keep the old hand in, little buddy," he told me. "Want me to fix you up with her roommate? Maybe we could party together sometime." I almost had to laugh when I realized Jack had slipped his hand inside his jacket and was stroking his little stub-nosed thirty-eight. Even I knew something about phallic symbolism and transference. The waitress at Long John Silver's on East Main in Lexington was older than Jack by at least ten years, but she said no to him anyway. Her husband was in town. Still, he was cheerful.

"One out of three is not a bad average," he told me. "Besides, it gives me a chance to save a little something for the little wifey! It's the uniform," he confided to me. "About one woman out of fifteen or twenty will spread for anything that wears a uniform. Authority figures. Same goes for suits and ties — money's the ultimate authority. That's what makes this drug war so deadly serious. Hell, the Kennedys got their start smuggling liquor during Prohibition and one of them became president. Money is power, boy. Don't you ever forget it."

"Don't leave home without it," I laughed, recalling the Karl Malden commercial for traveler's checks.

"Can't leave home without it." He swung the Crown Victoria to the right around the corner of a tall white bank building and stopped for a light a block further. At the second light, he bore left past a Catholic school and there was the Federal Building, facing Barr Street and shouldering up to Limestone. Jack swung onto Limestone Street, then into the parking lot that laid between the building and another short street called Pleasant Stone.

"We're here," he told me, as we went up the steps into the buff stone building. "Last chance to change your mind." The way he said it told me he didn't expect an answer. I followed him into the elevator and pressed the down button. In a few minutes, we were deep into the limestone layer that Lexington rests on. We walked into an unmarked office and a tall, Ichabod Crane-type behind the metal desk looked at his wristwatch.

"You're late," was his first comment, and Jack looked at his watch.

"Two minutes and eighteen seconds," he answered.

"What's your excuse?" He turned those dead-carp eyes on me and I looked him up and down the way I always do someone when I first meet them. Try to estimate what your enemy has — and everyone's a potential enemy. Jack ignored his question.

"This is Duncan O'Finioan, and Duncan, this is Albert Richards. He is our, uhm, coordinator."

I started to offer my hand, but then saw Richards wasn't interested.

"Raise your right hand. Do you solemnly swear to uphold the laws of the Constitution of the United States of America?"

"I do."

Richards nodded his head and grunted something.

"Sign these then and Miss Jenkins will issue your temporary ID and badge. You'll be contacted about your training."

"That's it?" I asked

"You want a brass band and fireworks?" Richards shot back. "Get the hell out of my office. I have work to do." He said as way of dismissing us.

Shit, what a prick, I thought. Damn, was I right!!

An hour later I was back in the Crown Victoria carrying papers that proved I was an Officer of the United States Department of Justice. First, though, I had been taken even deeper into the limestone layer into a sub-basement that is never, ever publicized. Here I was shown an armory or arsenal, whatever you want to call it. I looked over racks of M-16s and AK-47s, Colts and Smiths and

Uzis and Ingrams. It was the Ingram that caught my eye when Jack said, "Choose your weapons."

As I have said, I had fired an Ingram MAC-10 before, and that was my weapon of choice. MAC-10 is a forty-five caliber. My second choice was a standard Colt .45 automatic. For a backup, I picked a snub-nosed .44 Mag. Miss Jenkins was writing on a steno pad as I indicated to each one.

"You'll be assigned these weapons on completion of training," she told me, and locked my selections back in their cases. I felt like the king of the hill as I trotted back up the stairs and out onto the pavement. A whole new life was about to open up for me, and I could take on a whole platoon of dope dealers (Can you believe what a stupid ass I was?)! But little did I know my nightmare was about to begin.

CHAPTER 6

"Well, little buddy," Jack said as he wheeled the LTD into noon traffic. "What do you feel like eating?"

"Chinese," I told him. Lexington was supposed to have a fair Chinese restaurant or two, something that's rare east of the Bluegrass.

"Hunan, then." Jack wheeled onto Upper Street, crossed Main and turned east on Vine. Vine angles back when it reaches East Main, and in the Lexington streets, changes its name when it crosses Main. It then becomes Midland until it joins East Third to form Winchester Road. You swing off Winchester Road onto Liberty road till you hit New Circle. There a right shoots you down past Young Drive to Palumbo and you're practically there.

Just beyond Druthers is Hunan Palace. In a former life, it was known as Breedings and was host to a country-style group called Exile. As I was to hear later from a fellow Irish-American I hadn't met yet, "The essence of change is change."

I remember three things about that mid-afternoon meal. One was the food; prepared in a way only a good Asian chef can prepare it. I stuffed myself shamelessly on Jack's expense account. The second was a Japanese waitress that Jack kept hitting on. The third was the sake. I proceeded to get drunk on sake, after which I began to hear other words in place of the "Ah so!" the slender Japanese was using.

Once when Jack's hand cupped her round buttocks, I swear the

"Ah so!" came out a flat "Asshole!" I didn't think Jack would have wanted me to hear that, so I pretended to be drunker than I was, and I never remembered it in his presence. After all, he was the man who had just recruited me to kill people. I didn't want him to recruit someone else to save him embarrassment by taking me out. Not this early in the game anyway.

I let him help me back into the Crown Victoria, and had a nap while he cruised east. At Richmond, he looked up the E.K.U coed again. His K.S.P uniform was a passkey to the girl's room and his "investigation" lasted nearly an hour and a half. When he woke me up he was in a better mood. I guess his let down little ego was restored.

By the time we reached London, Jack was back up to his old standards, but the little redhead was off work. He shrugged and adjusted his sunglasses as he laughed. "One out of three ain't bad, 'specially when all you have got time for is a quickie. Ah, the pressures of duty!" Only he pronounced it "dooty." In Eastern Kentucky we still put the dyou sound in it, and think the dooty pronunciation is a big-city lapse, the kind that foreigners and town-class folks make.

I'd known Jack long enough to know he wasn't a big-city boy, though he liked to pretend he was. He liked to pretend he was a lot of things he wasn't. But whatever he pretended, he surely did have success with girls. Or at least with the waitresses. Some of them, anyway. And I always wondered if he ever scored with that little snub-nosed redhead.

I hope he did. I hope she gave him herpes.

Like a lot of things, I knew better than to ask. I'd already asked him about my training and he'd told me, "Soon enough, in this heat." I took that to mean I was in for some strenuous heavy-duty training. Maybe something that would make the logging camps or one of Danny Lane's black-belt classes look tame. Sounded like fun. What it actually turned out to mean was that Jack didn't know when I would be called up.

"Look," he told me, "You were picked for this job because I picked you for this job (I knew that was a lie). I recruit, they train."

He slipped his hand across his sunglasses and resettled them on his nose again. "And I picked you because you can shoot the shit out of someone and smile. Don't ever try to kid me, Duncan. You're the man-killer every grown man wishes he could be. And you just became a real-life double oh seven. Only you kill whom we point to. Now, your training in Virginia is going to be long and tough. Don't think it's not. If they have to break you first, they will. They're pros and they are tough!"

Ain't nobody going to break me, I thought. I may let them think they have. I wondered if the Shaolin boys remembered that fact. "You shot your first man when you were fifteen," he went on, "And your father covered for you. No one could ever prove otherwise, but we know it's true. And so does that guy from Baltimore. And we believe there have been at least two others since. Now, don't go feeling for that piece you're not carrying. If you weren't the kind who could kill, we wouldn't want you."

Actually, it was four men I had sent to a faraway place. But who was counting?

"Relax, you're going to shoot people and bring down a thousand dollars a week. That'll open a lot of slots in these Baptist hills."

Thank goodness, I thought. I was not going to be stuck in these Baptist hills ... at least not without a way out.

My way out came ten days later when Jack dropped by my class and told me to be ready to ship out at five the next morning (these jackwagons and five a.m., I tell you ...). He picked me up at my Inez school, again in the white Crown Victoria. This time he stopped only for coffee at London. Coffee and a half-hearted hit on the redhead whom he called Sandy. Then he took only an hour and ten minutes to set me in the front terminal building at Bluegrass Fields. An hour later, I was on a flight to Virginia Beach.

When I landed in Virginia Beach, I was picked up by a pair of semi-friendly men in the uniforms of Virginia state troopers. At this point, I was lost. Nobody told me where I was going and I didn't ask, though Langley was mentioned. The two troopers drove me out of town to some place I could not find on a roadmap. On a broad street at the edge of this town, the driver pulled over to the curb.

"Did anybody tell you, you have to be blindfolded for this leg of the trip?" the other asked me.

That didn't seem like too good a treatment for somebody you had high hopes for and I guess the thought showed in my face and I told them so!

"Relax, kid," the driver told me. "We don't even know where you're going ourselves, and we don't care to guess, much less go there. But we do ferry a number of men to this chopper pad and we ferry a few washouts back. We do know it's a top-secret operation, see? And what you don't know, you can't give away. You can't tell what you don't know, okay?"

What he said made sense, and I let the other trooper slip a blindfold on me. Only it wasn't your regular blue bandana-type blindfold that might attract attention. What I got was a modified pair of eye protectors with foam cushions all around and silvered lenses. I couldn't see the sun through them. Totally opaque.

What I judged was about an hour later, we paused and I heard a faint creak of gate hinges. A minute before we stopped, I heard the whoosh of helicopter blades. We crossed a stretch of driveway covered with fine gravel. When we stopped, the driver said "Good luck, boy," and the other trooper guided me to the chopper.

Once I was inside, he placed my duffel in my hand and strapped me in. Before we lifted off, I heard the sound a car turning in gravel makes, and then I was alone with my blindfold, feeling the warm July sun on the left side of my face.

After five or six minutes, I felt the sun's rays move across the other side of my face. I knew we were flying in circles. As I noticed on our first turn, we made five or six circles in the next half hour or so. I'd dropped four thousand feet without a parachute. And right about then, dropping four thousand feet without a chute was very much on my mind. I kept my mouth shut until I was in barracks and someone else had removed the blindfold.

I blinked against the bright Virginia sun and walked to an army-issue cot that was pointed out to me by someone who looked like a drill instructor. I learned later he wasn't. Just a prick.

"That's your bunk," he told me. "And there's your duffel. You'll find your clothing and gear in order. Training starts at oh-five-hundred in the morning."

He threw me a half salute and walked out. At the door, he paused. "There's a strict no fraternization rule imposed on your outfit. You're restricted to base, and you will send and receive no mail. Some don't need that long and some never make it out. Alive. Good luck." He was gone before my eyes adjusted enough for me to start examining my equipment.

The standard issue duffel bag held fatigues, cap and boots. A smaller bag contained the MAC, extra magazines, the Colt .45, its extra magazine, and tucked into a pocket inside the belt holster was the forty-four Mag backup piece. All were supplied generously with ammunition. Suddenly I felt much more secure. Then I saw the name stenciled on the duffel bag, and had to chuckle. Archie Bunker. It was the only piece of humor I found in the whole camp.

CHAPTER 7

Oh-five-hundred the next morning didn't come particularly early for me. By that time, I was usually halfway through my daily five-mile run, so I was wide awake when they turned us out.

By noon, I was loafing. My early physical training and the work in the logging camps had toughened me. Hell, I ran five every day, rain or shine. My twelve years in the martial arts had quickened me. Danny Lane had taught me well. My lifetime as an outcast had hardened me. Without boasting, I can say there was little they could teach me about weaponry.

On a bad day, I could shoot two eighty-five, and on a good day, two-ninety was easy. One of my brightest tasks was to take out a car with a twelve-gauge shotgun, at a range of forty yards. I'm not going to tell you how it's done, but I did it on one magazine load using a trick I had learned from my grandfather when I was a kid, who, by the way, was part of the founding of the IRA in Northern Ireland.

My instructor watched me and muttered something that sounded like "Goddamned terrorist." But he smiled when I slipped a couple more rounds into the magazine and jacked one into the chamber, giving him a very serious look.

The other things my Pop had taught me could turn the toughest soldier into a crying piece of shit in five minutes. Pop taught me how to survive. My physical training was cut short when I demonstrated my proficiency at the net and rope. Their calisthenics, forget about them. Try working a heavy bag for an hour, then drop and do a hundred push-ups. I did it every day. Some of my instructors could only shake their heads when I dropped into a full side split, put my chest on the ground and took a nap. Teach me how to fight? Hells bells, my father, my Pop and Danny Lane had taken care of that years earlier.

My firearms training was canceled when I consistently out-shot my instructor. This is not bragging. My expertise was simply the natural result of what amounts to a lifetime of handling weapons.

Let me pause here for a moment and explain my history with firearms. I was being trained to shoot by the time I could walk. My Pop, when he got to this country from Ireland, got work as a "trick shot" in a circus. He was undoubtedly the best pistol shot I have ever seen. I will always remember the mornings, well before daybreak, when he would get me up to target shoot. I vividly recall my asking him, "How the hell am I supposed to see the targets?" "See with your mind, not your eyes," he always told me, in that soft Irish brogue, then slapped me on the back of the head.

Then there was my father. A quick draw champion. No shit. He won one in Las Vegas. He had incredible speed, and he taught me that speed. He had a game he used to play with me. Dad stood behind me and would throw gravel out over my head to come down in front of me. Yep, you guessed it. I had to draw, shoot, hit the gravel and re-holster in one solid motion. Damn, I hated it when he tossed four and five of those gravel pieces at once.

My handgun skills were put to the test when I was but fifteen years old. I became involved in a shootout in the parking lot of a motel in downtown Inez. I did not, repeat, did *not* go for my weapon first. He did, and he will remain nameless here. But I did beat him on the draw, and two shots I fired hit their mark, and my target went down hard. So, here I was, being trained to shoot by people I wouldn't bet my left nut on, who had never had a target shoot back at them.

I have but one thing to say about that. Horse shit! There was only one area where I wasn't considered proficient — all my interpersonal relationships. That is, my man-to-man encounters have been based on the idea of winning. I had tested my strength against the tall tress of the Appalachians, and my speed and nerves against more than one man, and I had won.

For reasons I have always believed, it was better to kill than die, and better to get on with the killing than to pussyfoot around. I had signed on to hunt drug dealers and that was when the problems with my training came in. Actually, the one little thing they taught me was how to make drug buys. And I have to admit, that was the hardest thing I had to learn. To me, the object of the game was to take out the dealer. I still believe that, but I had to learn to do it their way.

Somewhere along the way, someone tacked the name "Hammer" on me. I don't know whether it was a code name or just a nickname. Anyway, it was what I was called, and what I'm still called when the Company contacts me. No one outside the Company calls me that.

But I started to tell you about my training as an undercover operator. It went something like this: I had to learn to act higher than the son of a bitch who was selling to me. When you have contempt for drug dealers as I did, that can be difficult, even in role-playing, play-acting, whatever you want to call it.

I met this limo — confiscated in a raid operation, I presumed — under a street light where two imaginary streets met. Unlike the TV pimp with his broad hat and inevitable fur-collared coat, mine wore a good cloth striped suit and a narrow brimmed hat that shaded the upper part of his face.

"What you lookin' for down here, white boy?" he asked me, as I walked up to his car. "Snowballs or meat?"

"How's the pussy trade?" I asked him.

"Hairy, as always," he came right back.

"But that's not the nature of the commodity." He visibly relaxed. "Now how much you want?"

"Shit, man, I'm horny. I figure three girls, at least." (Hey, this is the way I was taught to talk, okay?)

"Later, maybe," he laughed, skipping into the role of the dealer who had been out at ease. "I can slip you half a key if you got big ones."

"Was there a drought in the snow fields?" I asked him. "It's only ten a key in Florida, and thirty brought up."

"But this ain't fuckin' Florida, man," he grinned, "And there's a lot of state cops and judges between here and there. Besides, half a key's the same risk as ten keys. And you're not buying in bulk. Now show me the fucking money or take a fucking walk."

I pulled out my shirttail and worked the canvas money belt out. The shirttail dropped over the butt of my forty-four. My "dealer" riffled through the two hundred bills I showed him, and then reached under the car seat for a plastic bag. When I saw the white powder, the role-playing was over.

Three blank rounds from my forty-four burned holes in his shirt, right over his heart.

"Fucking shit!" he screamed as he slapped at his smoking clothes. Then my instructors were all around.

"No! No! Hell, no! Hammer," someone shouted. "You don't kill them. You just set them up and we arrest them. If they try to run, you clothesline them but don't shoot them unless they are shooting at you!"

Yes. I failed that test.

And the following two.

The next one also.

The next half dozen or so, too.

When I could finally talk with one of the dealers without seeing my brother's face, my trainers began to relax. That took about ten days. Between training sessions, they let me run with a ninety-pound pack on my back and use the modern-style gym they had set up. In the meantime, I had to sit through films and tapes of all my "buys" and hear that "No! No! Fucking no! Hammer!" each time I screwed up. I guess it worked. I stopped shooting them, at least for the duration of training.

Early on, I had noticed a tall redheaded fellow strolling about in a green beret atop a full Army major's uniform. I'd wondered who this peckerwood was, but our paths never crossed and like everything else that had nothing to do with my training, I knew better than to ask. I saw him at a couple of the re-runs of my training failures. Then one morning I met him face to face. Or side-to-side, I guess I should say.

As I've already said, I was allowed to run the mile track under full pack, and that is where I met him. So there I was, jogging along in full pack and combat gear while my instructors were trying to decide what to do with me next. I rounded the bend in the track and a shadow joined mine on the ground. I don't know whether he came up behind me or just materialized out of the air. I glanced to my right and there he was, that big peckerwood in the green beret, only this time he was wearing sweatpants, a sweatshirt and running shoes. He was running as easily as I was, but then, he was running bare and I was under an eighty-pound pack. At the time, I thought that was why he stayed with me so easily.

"Mind if I join you?"

"Suit yourself," I shot back, breathing heavily. After a few yards he spoke.

"You're good," was all he said.

I knew that, so I didn't bother to answer him (I know, I'm a tad bit arrogant, too). After a score of yards, he went on. "I think you would be a big asset once you get your head on straight. You're still too eager and too direct. Basically, you're still too inflexible in your approach. You may have curbed your instincts to take out the other party, but that's only in training. You know that this other guy's really on our side. But how will you react in the real world where there's no pretending, no play acting?" I didn't answer. I was thinking, Shit! Just what I need. Another dad.

"I think I know what you'll do," he went on. "And you do, too. We'll talk later." He put on a burst of speed from his long legs and left me. I knew that even without that eighty-pound pack I couldn't have kept up. I was glad he was gone; he was making me look bad. Next time I saw him, he was chatting with one of my instructors and I knew I was the subject of the discussion.

My second direct encounter with him came on the firing range when I emptied the magazine of my MAC-10 into those pop-up targets skipping over the old man with a cane who was thrown in to test our decision speed. The redhead was nodding approvingly. "You got it," he told me. "Hold the weapon firmly enough for accuracy but let it wander enough to get a shotgun effect."

Just for the hell of it, I snapshot the old man's silhouette with my forty-five. The redhead grinned.

"We've got a group going," he told me. "Or actually, we're assembling a new group, a squad, call it what you will, that can make use of your undeniable, if inadmissible, talents. Can you shoot anybody who is pointed out to you as a target?"

"I have," I told him. "People that needed it." The major chuckled, and walked away shaking his head.

A week later, he was back. An instructor whose name I was never told called me to the head of an otherwise empty room. "Hammer," he said, "I want you to meet Major Sean O'Shaunessey. He thinks you and he have something to talk about." The instructor threw Sean a sloppy salute, glanced coldly at me and left the room. Asshole.

This was at the end of our intensified training programs. For five days, we had outdone the rangers for sheer gruesome scheduling. We learned to sleep during roll call and during briefings. Nap when you can, but come alert at the unanswered sound of your name.

I was dead on my feet. All part of the game, I told myself, knowing there were worse tortures. For the past day and a half, I'd been reliving my own self-imposed rite of passage into manhood.

"You shot a man when you were fourteen or fifteen, didn't you?"

When you're totally exhausted, you answer more honestly than you will when you're totally shitfaced. They know that. And I do too, now. I've used it a few times myself.

"Yeah, but how the fuck did you know that?" I asked.

"We have our ways," Major O'Shaunessey answered, with just a trace of amusement.

"Well, yeah, no problem. I shot him, and I've done one or two more since then, too." I said you get totally honest when you're exhausted.

"Well, I've got a proposition for you."

"Okay, what? Can it beat a thousand dollars a week?" I asked him.

"No," he answered, "Still pays the same, but the risks aren't quite as bad. I need a co-captain."

I said, "Okay. I don't care. Just give me twelve hours sleep."

"If you're in, you've got it," he told me, "and if you're not, you'll take it anyway. Here's the deal: You may have noticed there are two types of men being trained here. Men like you, whom we hope to keep around for a while. A killer, if you will. And then there is the rank and file that will work on a need-be basis — come and go." I found out later that most of the men were mostly go. As in going, going, gone. Get the hell off the stage kind of gone.

My grandfather had a saying. "Might as well hang for a sheep as for a lamb," I recited.

"There's little danger of hanging," he grinned. "But there is some of being shot, stabbed or burned, or simply being beaten half or all the way to death."

It turned out he was wrong on only one account; in my three years with the Unicorns, I was shot and stabbed repeatedly. Once I was hung up by my wrists and had the living shit beaten out of me. And remember, being co-captain brought less risk than the other Unicorns fighting. Yeah, right.

CHAPTER 8

Herman Rosen was the only Jewish boy I knew in Inez, and when he was thirteen he went away to his Bar Mitzvah in Louisville. Lou-a-vil, we called it, like most Kentuckians, or just Lui-Vil. Anyway, I asked Herman what it meant and he said it meant he was a man now in the eyes of his faith. But he seemed a little embarrassed to talk about it, like it was too personal to mention — or maybe too old-fashioned.

I knew enough not to press him for details, but his account stirred in me something I preferred to think of as an ancestral longing. Probably it was more the stories I had read about. Indian manhood initiation ceremonies. I let my Indian blood make the decision. Also, because at that time in my life, I had not yet learned enough of my Irish/Celtic/Norse blood to know what to do with it. I think that part of my family's history was kept hidden from me as long as possible.

After all, my grandfather and his family were chased from the Island by the British for being part of the IRA, a fact I would come to know and appreciate, even learn to use. My guess was my father and Pop feared that as soon as I became of age, I would run off to Ireland and join the fight. If they only knew what I was doing now. Up the IRA!

Anyway, for now, my Cherokee blood is what I called upon. I was a tad bit younger than Herman and hadn't yet started working the logging operation with my father. That was to come a year and a half in the future, and it was still late summer, so I wasn't in school. I wandered over to the creek and stared at the clouds reflected in the water as I tried to remember all I knew of the American Indian rites of passage. Being only twelve, I was a little sorry that taking a scalp was not part of the proof of manhood. That, my mother had insisted, was not really the Cherokee way but had been introduced by the white man as a method of keeping score at a time when a bounty was paid for each Indian killed.

I remember thinking "What a shame." I had a couple people I really would have liked to scalp. School chums, you know. She also said these hills were red with Cherokee blood before the white man came.

"We were the Jews of North America," she said. "Though we didn't know what a Jew was, and we called the land simply 'the land.' The Mississippi was our Red Sea and it didn't part for us. Many died at the crossing, and when the white man came, we were almost at the Sea and only a hundred Cherokee were left from each of the tribes of Israel. The Indians were humans without ships, cannons or even a musket. We would do what France and England and Holland could do: die at one another's hands.

"It's a primary power, son. It's not always the strong that survive. It may be the quick. As painful as it is to watch friends and family die, the survivors have a better chance of coping with a hostile world. No other Indian nation adopted the white man's ways as the Cherokee did, and no other tribe produced a Sequoia who turned a whole nation literate in a single year. "But remember to grab the gold, son. Without gold, there would have been no Trail of Tears."

My mother was always bitter about the Trail, the way some Southerners are bitter about another event that happened about two decades later. Anyway, about the Trail of Tears: The army did such a good job of moving the Cherokee nation to Oklahoma that there are Cherokees in Georgia, Tennessee and the Carolinas to this day. But I was telling you about my self-instilled Bar Mitzvah, or rather my personal coming of age ceremony.

Part of it was word of mouth stuff, but mostly it was what I read, and I am afraid it came out more Cheyenne than Cherokee. But what the hell, right? Whatever works. First I would need a high place, I knew that. A high place might have had some symbolism in the plains, but over here in Eastern Kentucky, they were so plentiful as to be a nuisance. But I had a particular one in mind anyway. It jutted into the bend of a creek and rose seventy or eighty feet straight up from a little pool that couldn't have been more than two feet deep in the summer.

I told my mother I was going on one last camping trip before school started and packed up my camping gear. A mile outside of town I stashed my kit and headed for my high place. This was about ten in the morning. Dew was still glittering in places of deep shadow among the rocks, pines, and cucumber trees.

My plan was simple. I intended to circle around to my high place and edge out onto the top of the rock. I would build a shelter with my bare hands by stripping off pine and hemlock boughs. Then I would sit back and wait for my vision. I had read that burning sweet grass was part of the Cheyenne ritual, but hell, I didn't know sweet grass from Kentucky fescue, so I settled on spearmint instead. As an inhalant, I don't think it will ever replace burly tobacco or sandalwood incense.

Anyway, there I was, atop a rocky outcropping, shaded by a scraggly pine tree and sheltered by a so-so lean-to that smelled as sweet as a room full of deodorant. By mid-afternoon I was sitting in my shelter, feeling my ass go numb from the rock. All the dew was dried up by now and I was remembering what an August afternoon in the Kentucky hills can be like. The heat can beat down from the sky like it was coming from the lamps they use to keep food warm. It can also radiate up from the ground like it was coming from one of those stoves they use to cook the food before setting it under the lamps to dry out. Inside a shelter, even one with a side open, it can reach from a hundred to a hundred and ten degrees.

As I was about to doze off, I remembered that some tribes used a sweat lodge to encourage the vision; hell, I didn't need one. By three in the afternoon, if my reckoning was right, my whole world was a sweat lodge, and the sweat bees found me. Not just the little buzzing kind, but also the big, green, ugly kind, long as a joint of my finger.

Now, everyone knows that the sweat bee is a peaceful little creature. They will sit there and drink your sweat or suck your salt or whatever the hell it is the ugly little bastards take from you and never bother you unless they are touched by something — and they have a way of crawling into your sleeves like they were meant to be touched and given an excuse.

I first became aware of them when I dozed off and my head dropped onto my chest. I woke up damned fast! Stings will do that to you. Three bees had crawled down the front of my neck and got caught in the creases of my neck when I nodded forward. I killed the two little ones while they were confused; but the big-ass bastard got away. There may be a space for all creatures great and small, but folded into a twelve-year-old's neck creases ain't one of the safer places.

An hour later, the ants found me. Big black creatures like little pieces of glassy, shiny night, walking up my thighs and taking an occasional bite. After a few dozen got swatted, the others were occupied with the bodies they could carry off and sort of left me alone. By the time it was really sundown and the mosquitoes were venturing out from the underside of the leaves of the trees; I was glad it had been dry for a while. Ticks were about all I needed to round out my insect plague — or maybe locusts! By this time I was expecting lions, tigers and bears. Oh my.

I finally got an idea. I piled my supply of mint around my fire and got a lot of smoke. That helped, and I was able to doze again, despite a trio of jays that were squawking and frolicking in the trees above my head. Off over to my left I could hear the seasonal cough of a shotgun — squirrel season was open — and despite the mountain man's legendary skill with the rifle, he rarely bothered to take the risk of missing. After all, the country hunter is usually a meat hunter and not a sportsman. The sound, though, reminded me that I had not eaten today.

I could taste gray squirrel simmered in gravy. Gravy sopped up with hot buttered biscuits and washed down with cold, sweet milk. But I wasn't really hungry. Yet. Picturing that meal was really a sort of idea daydream. Sort of like word association, after hearing the shotgun hunter.

By the next morning, there was a definite hollow feeling beneath my loincloth and my throat was a little dry. Things didn't change much in the next two days, except the swarming bugs had told all their kinfolk and acquaintances that I was there. Bastards. And the bats and the bull bats (I hate bats!) moved in to squeak and swoop among the smaller creatures. A shower on the second day had sent water running through my roof and into my mouth, but by the third day, I was definitely having visions.

I had visions of Pepsis and milkshakes. In the afternoon, I was visited by the spirit of the Coke float, then lemonade. I woke from that one to the sound of a bullfrog leaping into the pool eighty feet beneath my perch. That invoked visions of frog legs rolled in corn meal and fried in beef fat with fried potatoes and thick slices of ripe fat yellow tomatoes my mother liked to grow. I was conscious enough to know there was water eighty feet below me; I was smart enough to know it was undoubtedly polluted. Telling myself that the water was rife with germs let me get back to sleep.

I got my vision the next morning. Whether from exhaustion or some other reason, I slept till past midmorning. By now, I wasn't even feeling the bug bites. The sweat bee stings still managed to attract my attention, though.

I woke to the image of Death. Death in red and black, staring with a bright eye into my face, and reeking of the grave, or at least of decay. The mottled head of a turkey buzzard was gone with an oily swish of wings. He just flopped backwards over the edge of the cliff and was gone. My head swayed, and I dreamed that I was on an endless and fatal jaunt, patrolling the skies for fresh pools of water while black and glossy clouds, shot with the oily fire of sunset, boiled and tumbled in the background. Somehow, I was a compound of the earth spirit, and of wild freedom and of the inevitability of the grave, whether it is of earth or of flesh.

The trouble was, I didn't recognize my vision at the time. I just took it for a bad dream brought on by hunger and thirst and the fright of staring into the emotionless red-set eye that had found me not quite sufficiently dead.

My father found me later that day and got me dressed in my regular clothes before he took me home. He told my mother some tale of finding me sick in the hills. "Some kind of fever," he reckoned, but my mother looked long at me and nodded in the way she had that let us know she knew she was being lied to — protected. A long time later, she casually mentioned that a warrior, like a dreamer, needed a shaman, an analyst to interpret his vision. It was a decade and a half later before that black and red image came back to me.

CHAPTER 9

"This is your first assignment, so don't worry about seeming nervous," Jack had told me. "You're a kid, scoring from a new connection, so you are bound to be anxious. The feds have to see you make the buy and the stuff change hands. When they yell 'Halt,' you split. Simple enough. You have had the best training money can buy; you know the scenario. So let's go to work."

I nodded and got out of Jack's Lincoln, well out of sight of our target. Jack wouldn't be seen near — nor be involved directly in — the actual bust. As the brown Lincoln purred out of sight, I checked the little piece in my pocket and unsnapped the flap of my folding belt-knife pouch. "Hell," I told myself. "You're just damn nervous, jittery."

Jack's Lincoln was long gone by the time I sauntered up to the corner where one of the mountain's Holbrooks was supposed to be dealing. If this guy was a Holbrook, and lived east of Richmond, he had to be kin to the gas company Holbrooks of Martin County, as far as I knew. But those bastards are a whole other story. This set of Holbrooks had been big in growing tobacco, but may have moved into marijuana farming. With their state police connections, the fields would have been safe. And this one could have used a hay baler to make his pot fit into the trunk of those gray LTDs.

I moved up the street till I spotted my target. He had the bony cheeks and the dark eyes of the Martin county Holbrooks, though his hair was almost straw-blond. But he had that same better than anyone else, nose in the air, dumbass look. He was maybe two or three years older than me, with what I have since come to recognize as the arrogance of youth. Arrogant recklessness, I should say. Or maybe just plain fucking stupid.

I watched him contact three or four people, one in the uniform of a sheriff's deputy, before I caught his eye. He held my gaze until I remembered to look away. When I looked back, he caught my eye again. As I have said, I didn't have to fake nervousness. My tongue was as dry as if I had been smoking a tinder pot, and my eyes ached from shifting too many directions in too limited a space.

Finally, I squared my shoulders and strolled directly up to him. "I'll be damned!" I said to myself. I recognized him as one of the Holbrooks who was two or three years ahead of me at good old Sheldon Clark High. About the time I dropped out, he had graduated and left town. The local paper, always short on printable news, had run a short story with his picture. The story told how Ron Arnett Holbrook had graduated with honors and would immediately leave for Lexington to attend the University of Kentucky. The caption under the picture had begun, "To Seek Degree." I wondered if the hometown boy would get the third degree after today.

"Hey, Duncan!" he called as I walked up. I was surprised and disconcerted that he remembered my name. "Don't be shy! Come on up. How is the old hammer hanging?"

When I hesitated, he urged me, "Hey, like I said, don't be shy. I never knew you liked to smoke, but I sold a ton of this shit to your little brother. Say, you're smart to buy away from home, though. What the local yokels don't know about you can't hurt you. Right?"

That remark about selling to my brother sealed the bastard's fate. I wanted nothing more at that moment than to take my weapon, ram it up Mister Holbrook's ass, and shoot until it was empty. But I allowed him to go on talking.

"Don't guess I've seen you to talk to you since I went to college, have I? Don't ever go to college, man. You never saw such a stuck-up pile of shits as there are in Lexington, and all as innocent as hell, to hear them tell it."

And I bet you fit right in, you stack of shit, I thought to myself. He kept on talking.

"I hooked up with this dealer," he continued, "Named Berkins, and we served a party at that big place on Winchester Road. He brought an old guy from Lawrenceburg with him to count the money, and he quit at one 'o clock. Said his fingers were tired from counting hundred dollar bills. Shit! Even the fucking governor was there! Nickel, dime, or quarter?"

The sudden casual switch from bragging to selling caught me off-guard, but I said "Two dime," and eased a rolled twenty into his pocket, the way I had been told he liked done. Later I wondered if that was so he could pretend to himself he had found the money, or that it had mysteriously appeared. I, in turn, got two partially-filled plastic sandwich bags dropped into my jacket pocket as Holbrook slapped me on the back and let his hand slide down. Like a snake crawling, it made me want to puke, kick the shit out of him, and then puke some more.

"I'm in pretty tight with the cops," he told me. "But you're from out of town. Pays to be careful, you know. You know," he repeated to himself in another tone. "Those assholes in Lexington got strange ideas, man, some of them anyway. That University built a great Memorial Coliseum to commemorate the boys who died in World War Two, and they put all their names up inside, cased in the building. Yards and yards of fucking scrolls with all the names of the boys on the paper. But they got the names of the asshole fucking U.K. basketball players engraved in bronze stones. How's that for priorities? Man, talk about a kick in the ass.

"And old Coach Rupp, who made a fortune fixing games for Fred Kern, the biggest gambler in town — Lexington built a multi-million dollar stadium and called it Rupp Arena! Hell, there are people around who will tell you how he teamed up with the gamblers and then let the players take the fall. The beauty of it was that he could do it without losing a game.

"Point spread! That's the secret. That's the way to beat the old conscience. Win all your games and keep your reputation, just don't beat the other team by as much as you ought to. On a salary of a few thousand dollars a year the old rogue became a millionaire landowner in the Bluegrass. And those suckers on his team would do anything for him, even take the fall. Man, that's taking team spirit to the limit. The dumbass fuckers."

I had reached into my jacket pocket as he was rambling on and pulled out the two small bags, tossing them from one hand to the other. I hoped he thought I was eager to smoke the stuff. By now, he seemed to have talked himself into a strange sort of friendship with me. He finally changed the subject, which was good, because I really couldn't care less about Kentucky basketball, or basketball, period. To put it mildly, I hate the fucking game.

"Duncan," he said, "I've got good stuff. The best the Daniel Boone National Forest can produce. But after talking to you again, I sort of hate to see you on this shit. Was it your brother that turned you on to it?"

The mention of my brother again started to make me even madder, and I squeezed the two bags together in my fist. But then Holbrook said softly, "Damn feds," and darted into the street. There was a squeal of brakes as the driver of a Camaro swerved to miss him. Then I took off, hearing the shout of "Halt! Federal officer!" behind me.

I took off down the side street as planned. The scenario was right on schedule. Only it was two feds who were coming up the alley. It was one fed and a dumbass Paintsville deputy. The fed was saying "Halt," as his part called for, and the Johnson County deputy was easing his pistol out of his holster. The fed said, "No shooting," and shoved the deputy before grabbing at me. As rehearsed, he got a hand on my left arm and I snatched it away. When I did so, the two plastic bags were snapped out of my hand. I pounded down the alley like Citation at the Belmont and as I turned, I heard the fed say, "No, damnit! No shooting. We got the stuff and we got the dealer. Let the kid go!"

That's how I came to know the feds were smart enough not to trust the local law. I am sure the feds were for sale, but no little street dealer was going to come up with what it took to buy them. Once around the corner, I slowed to a walk and turned back to watch this fed beat the local to my twenty bucks of pot. Then I sauntered away, hoping it was true you could hide in plain sight by changing your pace. To be safer, though, I reversed my windbreaker from blue to red. But I was still sweating as I eased onto a stool at the diner a block away.

At the trial a few weeks later, the bastard protected me in a perverse sort of way. He told the judge that I was a stranger trying to sell him two bags, which he didn't need since he had bought some earlier. It didn't get him off the hook, because the cops wanted him. But the bastard lived up to his name. I told myself he had the six months in La Grange coming to him. I had made it though my first time.

CHAPTER 10

About a year after my first assignment I was introduced to Nancy Cramer — or, as Richards called her, our new piece of transportation equipment. I watched that piece of transportation equipment walk out of the room while Richards was chasing a Hershey bar with the smoke from a Swisher Sweet cigar, and I shuddered. The Hershey bar is delicious and the Swisher Sweet cigar may be a fine cigar for those who like to smoke sugar, or molasses, or whatever it is they are sweetened with.

I don't know which gagged me, the combination of chocolate and Sweets, or the combination of chocolate, Sweets, and Richards. The guy was a damn spook in the worst sense of the word. His thin ascetic figure was a ghost of the survivor of the life we were living. To him, life had value only if the living could further the pursuit of his goal, the eradication of the illegal drug trade in the United States. He was close to my heart at that point at that time. I had seen a brother lured into the drug scene, and I knew I could kill anything that smelled of the white seduction. That is how I had come to think of coke peddlers by this time.

Where was I? The transportation equipment. As I watched the tiny perfect figure walk out of the room, I had only one thought: This was the most beautifully made woman I had ever seen. She differed only in hair color from the best-known perfect figure in the world. Playboy's feline had bleached her hair and had come obscenely to life on the briefing room wall where men or mythological creatures — who do not exist — were about to go out

73

to meet other living, breathing, existing creatures and bring an end to their existence. This was one piece of transportation equipment I wanted to get to know. Wanted as desperately as if I were a medieval master with an extensive holding and the arrogance to demand *droit de seigneur*. That was a term Sean had introduced me to: a fancy term for cherry picking, or, as he explained it, the first fuck.

She walked out as cool and confident as anything I had ever seen, and Richards went on sucking on first the candy bar, and then his cigar.

"Miss Cramer," he said, "will accompany the unit on its scheduled operation. Captain Breathitt's illness will prevent him from flying for awhile." He told the lie with an absolutely straight face, as if the five of us had not watched Captain Breathitt's "illness" cause him to slump forward at the controls of the Huey he was piloting and send it into a canted spiral that might have broken the bird's back and killed us all. Richards and Hemorrhoid, oh, sorry again, Jack, included, if I had not grabbed the stick and fought the savage to the ground.

I am a fair study with machinery, and I had been flying off and on for several years, but that type of situation was new to me. As it was, I couldn't reach the pedals at all, so the spiral continued. The throttle was so damn stiff, I brought the bird in at a very bad angle and sheared the north side branches off a thirty-foot Hemlock before I severed the tail rotor completely and dislocated the whole assembly.

The rest of us walked away limping and bruised, while Captain Breathitt of the Kentucky National Guard snored on deck. To make matters worse, his snores smelled of Scotch instead of good old Kentucky Bourbon. I must pause here and say this, because it comes straight from the bottom of my now-black heart. If I had known then what I do now, I swear, I would have let that damn chopper crash. But as fate would have it, my survival training had been very good. I saved us that day. I hope the Gods forgive me for that.

Breathitt's illness was a stroke of luck for us, if Nancy Cramer could fly the way she walked out of that room — smooth-assed and confident. I like that in a woman. Don't get me wrong; I am not a chauvinist, at least, not like most Kentucky men. Deep down in their hearts Kentucky men don't like to trust any woman with any machine more mobile than a Singer or a Maytag, though they have a grudging respect for one who has mastered the complexity of the hypodermic. As long as she functions under the eye of a male, who may not be able to tell mumps from shingles, but can still write M.D. after his name. But there I go, wandering off-track again.

The girl who had just walked out was no more than five foot three. She might have weighed a hundred and ten pounds, but it was all in the right places. She had everything: shimmering platinum hair, an incredible figure and absolute confidence that she had the attention and admiration of every male in the room — except Richards.

"The no fraternizing rule will, of course, apply here. Especially here." I noticed a smear of chocolate or amber or both at the right corner of his mouth. Jack had turned in his chair to watch her transport herself out of the room. By the time she was gone, I was transported too. The song "Fly Me to the Moon" began running through my mind. What a shame you couldn't get there in a chopper.

Suddenly, Sean got a mischievous look in his eye and gave a long moan. Another Unicorn glanced at him and laughed, then answered in kind. Jack came to his feet with a flushed face and a wet spot on his suit pants, just as Richards stepped to his desk and brought down a bony hand on the lectern.

"We are not here to reenact the moaning scene from Catch-22," he announced, and ruined the effect by slapping the desk beside the lectern. Jack glanced at him and nodded.

"You have seen pilots before," Jack said in a sucking up tone, "So if you don't want to be replaced now, show some respect."

"Begging your pardon, Jack," Sean said easily, "But I believe we were showing admiration for a piece of transportation equipment. Without reference to our sweet sucking leader here. And what a ride!" A Unicorn laughed and Richards became, what was for him, the highest of excited.

"Now," he went on, "What I have been trying to tell you bunch of bastards, if you need a ride in anything from a Skyhawk to a Sherman, or a HiPer Lite to a Hercules, for the time being Miss Cramer will be the person to see. If you want to know about a license number in Alaska or Europe, or the legitimacy of someone's second cousin's sorority sister, you tell Miss Cramer. She is as good with a computer as she is with transportation equipment." He talked on in his unemotional, peculiar way.

I already knew by the use of the title "Miss" that she wasn't married. Unmarried meant more likely available than married. Or more easy, though recently married often provides just the cover some women need. I already knew this wasn't one of them. I came alert to Richards in time to hear him say "... full tropical gear. With military air cover. You'll receive your packets on the plane." He nodded and left the room, trailed by Jack. And as usual, Jack's nose was buried deep up Richards's ass. A hemorrhoid knows a hemorrhoid. Sean was grinning at me as I turned.

"What did I miss?" I asked him. "I got to thinking of something else and lost track."

"Something," he grinned. "Parts of someone, possibly. But cheer up, me boy. He said we're going to have a holiday. A regular tropical vacation."

I left the briefing room with only one thought: The memory of that full blouse and those smooth designer jeans.

"Let me guess," Sean said as we left the room together. "You have fallen in lust at first sight."

CHAPTER 11

As the big Hurk Copter circled low over a city that was definitely not in Eastern Kentucky, I had an impression of buff tile, red and green. I saw endless undulating crowded green with here and there a ribbon of muddy water twisting through it. There were narrower straight ribbons of asphalt and still slimmer bands that looked like gravel or just plain old, rutted dirt. We still have enough roads like that in Eastern Kentucky that they look familiar even from twenty thousand feet.

"This is to be a surgical procedure," Richards had told us. "You will be dropped over your target, which you will then proceed to seize and destroy. Apache gunships will control the airspace and tend to radio jamming. You will maintain radio silence. No sense getting picked up by some local ham (like anyone there could afford that equipment). The gunships are strictly a military offering — our military — and so are not here. The local government will not see them, nor acknowledge their presence. To further facilitate their nonexistence, they will fly without insignias." Hmm, ever hear of black helicopters? Hee hee hee.

"The crop you are going after, identified by satellite photo courtesy of our friends in the CIA, is estimated to have a value of somewhere in the neighborhood of two hundred million dollars, American. That, boys and girls, could buy you a very nice Senate seat."

"It's more than a double fistful of dollars, too," Sean had added, without interrupting Richards.

"Call it a quarter of a billion dollars," Richards went on in a cold and bloodless way, without giving so much as a nod to Sean. Another man, I thought, would have capitalized the quarter of a billion. The way Richards pronounced it, it was only a rounded-off score. Come to think of it, it wouldn't buy too many of the machines we were using these days.

You think maybe there was more to burning this marijuana field than just getting rid of the dope? I sure as hell did, later. So, we parachuted from our transport plane into the midst of what well may have been one of the most cost-efficient farming operations in the history of agriculture. More green. Ten to fifteen feet high.

This particular mary jane, marijuana, cannabis sativa, was in orderly rows as neatly laid down as a field of Kentucky barley, or of Iowa corn, while on the low surrounding hills the jungle crowded in as if eager to reclaim the plot. I wondered if this jungle was different from our vegetation back home. Oh, I knew it was green year-round, but so were the pines back home and the other trees that shed their leaves could be just as impenetrable as these in their season.

Orange parachutes hummed down drums and boxes trailing green or orange smoke as we tried to hold together our descent. Five Unicorns hung in the air with machetes sheathed at one side and M-16s on the other. This was not going to be the kind of harvest Ceres would approve of. But then it never would have been.

Above, fourteen men in anonymous uniforms guided their parachutes in toward the faster-falling cargo chutes. I knew these were brown-skinned Latino types, and wondered if their identity would ever be known if they died here. I figured they would probably be unnamed volunteers in some minor revolutionary group if they were killed. Just before I dropped into pot over my head, I saw four anonymous helicopters whoop-whoop into sight and break formation to take up positions over various portions of the plantation.

One pilot must have been too eager or unthinking, or maybe just too damn stupid, for I saw one chute collapse from the down-wash of helicopter blades, then slide into a tree like a kid coming down a playground slide. First volunteer for that liberation army, I thought. Rest in peace. Then I stopped thinking.

My own chute was spread over two or three rows of pot, easily a thousand or fifteen hundred dollars worth. Almost to my left was an oil drum, standing with part of its end buried in the loose, well-tilled soil. I unsheathed my machete and slashed though clumps of stalks near the ground. In five minutes maybe ten thousand dollars worth of pot was stacked loosely across the rows of the field. Ten minutes after that the pile was higher than my head. I moved away to start another pile.

By the time the second pile was finished, Sean and another Unicorn had moved up and began piling stalks on my piles. We had nineteen men on the ground to begin with. Or rather, eighteen live men on the ground and one corpse (after we cut his ass down from that tree he hit) to destroy a quarter billion dollar crop. We did not plan to send up any smoke before we had at least half of it in piles. We were not counting the plants, but we figured there ought to be about half a million of them.

I guessed these plants were spaced about two meters apart, enough to let the tractors run through. This was one of those ideal little farms that had the cheap Latin American labor which enabled the owners to live like Asian despots with minimum outlay. The trouble with Asian despots is that they have to keep armies as well as peasants. If they can combine the two, so much the better. But whether part-time or full-time, armies have to be equipped — and this was a fairly modern setup.

I never knew who the honcho here was, but he had connections. Our first hint came when one of those multi-million dollar birds up there mushroomed into a fireball and parts of airframe, rotor, weapons and crew rained down. Then bloody hell broke loose.

The other choppers were taking evasive action, firing rockets and chain guns. An oily spout of flame told me they had scored on the fuel dump. In lulls of the firing, we heard jeeps roaring through the field. For some reason I glanced at my watch; we had been on the ground just under an hour. I wondered if Richards or the dumb fucks in the U.S. military had counted on surface-to-air missile defense.

Then the jeeps arrived. Sumbitch, we knew we were in deep shit! Two vehicles plunged into the clearing that we had made and they were regular army. But the wrong damned army! So were the men pointing M16s in our general direction.

Sean yelled, "We surrender!" as we both sprayed the first Jeeps with our Ingrams. A figure I took to be a captain pulled over sideways and both drivers tromped their gas pedals, trying to run for cover. Don't believe what you see on the TV, movies or on your X-Box — the spectacular fireball that comes from an explosive bomb in the gas tank doesn't usually happen the way they show. This one just whooshed and suddenly there were two burning figures rolling and screaming in the dirt.

"Fiesta time," Sean said softly, and fired a short burst into each figure. The captain was burning quietly, as was the fourth man in the Jeep who must have died when we first sprayed the car. My MAC-10 was chewing up pot as I tracked the escaping jeep, and the Latino soldier's M16 was chattering sharply.

In the next lull, we heard firing all over the area (where were Jack and Richards when you wanted them?). I heard M16s and .45s mostly, mixed with the distinctive rumbling chatter of Ingrams. At this point all the Unicorns seemed to be still functioning. I guess our air cover, already reduced by a fourth, did as much as they could, which wasn't much. I knew they took out the hacienda and a shitload of other buildings. Then they began hosing down the area where the firing was coming from, and those boys were mad. Rocket and machine gun fire sent pot and more body parts into the air. And more than once, US!

When we had nothing to shoot at, I finally remembered that the need for radio silence was over. I flipped the switch and heard one word: "Sabot," repeated over and over. Abort, fall back to rendezvous area to be picked up. Yeah, sure. With half the goddamned Guatemalan army sitting across our path and an angry pot farmer and HIS paid-for Army backing it up.

"We're screwed," Sean said philosophically. "Set up. Regular night of the Long Knives." I did not know what he was talking about, and right then I really didn't give a flying shit. All I knew was a bunch of very angry men, with a lot of guns, were shouting Spanish at us and also addressing us in the universal language — firepower.

As we reached the edge of the clearing — the jungle clearing, not the pot clearing — I saw the leg of Sean's camos twitch and begin to turn dark. He never slackened stride, but glanced back to give me a tight wouldn't-you-know-it grin. A few yards into the jungle, he paused and leaned against the bole of a tree, listening.

"That way lays the pick-up point," he said, "Which means that's where everybody else will lead, including our generous host. About five miles southeast of here, on the other hand, is a small clearing I spotted on the way in. You have you communicator and our backup chopper has hers, but if you call, know they'll be waiting when we get there, and she sure as hell can't put down on this little golf green. Oh, by the way, I think I may need some help before we get there." Then he pitched forward on his face.

When I turned him over, there was another hole by his left hip, and his black uniform was a dark bloody mess. I looked around for the Latino soldier, but we had gotten separated in the dash for the trees. Hell, he was probably halfway home by now. I slung Sean's MAC-10 to my left shoulder and stooped to try to bind his wounds. He roused enough to help me get his two hundred and thirty pounds onto my back. It never occurred to me to lighten the load by getting rid of his weapons and communicator. Sean was alive. That meant he needed them. Then, into the mouth of hell we went.

CHAPTER 12

Three days.

Three days in that damned jungle. I had never been so tired, so hungry, and so pissed off! The pain was secondary. Three days of eating bugs and roots. Three days of running with my friend on my back. Run, then hide. Run, then hide, trying to avoid a firefight I knew we would not win. But I had vowed, by God, either we both made it out alive, or neither of us did.

Suddenly, on the evening of the third day, the earpiece I was wearing burst into life. Right then I heard the voice of an angel. "Come on, you guys, dinner's getting cold." Nancy Cramer's voice told me over my earpiece, her voice high-pitched against the Huey's clatter. I looked around and saw the outline of the chopper coming straight at us out of the north. Sean and I just looked at each other and laughed.

"Trouble with working late," Sean told her through clenched teeth as we were climbing aboard the chopper, though she couldn't have heard, so his words were meant for me. "Makes you miss your dinner." I don't know how he knew the rest of the survivors of the squad had been lifted out, but I sensed something was troubling him. Something more than being "smitten hip and thigh." Something more than spending three days in that jungle. But right there as we lifted off, I was more interested in getting his wounds taken care of by someone other them me.

After getting Sean strapped in and padded as much as possible, I fell into the copilot's chair beside Nancy. She turned her face to me, smiling. "You ready to go?" she asked.

"Pedal to the metal, my angel," I said.

"You got it," she said, as she pointed us in the direction of a secret U.S. military base. With the throttle wide open, we flew over the jungle Sean and I had spent the last three days in. I hope I never see this place again, I thought to myself. 'Cause I swear if I do, I will nuke the damn place.

And Nancy, I later learned, was in trouble. Big, deep trouble. She was supposed to stay back at the jungle base and monitor radio traffic. The unmarked bird we flew out in had been commandeered hardware when Richards had refused to send in a rescue team for us.

I didn't see Sean after we left the jungle until his wounds were healed, several weeks later. He was incognito. Nancy and I, though, had a direct and blunt interview with Jack as soon as we got back to the States. This took place in the room that was kept for him in a motel in Paintsville. Paintsville is in Johnson County. A big hangout for corrupt judges of Eastern Kentucky.

"You were both insubordinate," he said bluntly. "Duncan, you did not follow orders and destroy the crop. Nancy, you deserted you post under fire and almost got three of you killed by hostile government forces." Nancy wasn't quelled.

"Looks to me like I pulled their asses out of a shitstorm of *your* making," she said.

"Appearances can be deceiving," he said in the coldest tone I had ever heard him use. I was too young to know how true those words were. To me, what you saw was reality. I hadn't yet equated delusion with hypocrisy. "As a result of your actions, the quarter billion dollar pot field is still there, tens of thousands have been expended in fuel and supplies and God knows how many men are dead. Now get out of here. I don't want to see or hear from either of you for at least a week."

Fine with me. I had other things on my mind. My shoulders and back were aching and sore from lugging Sean on my back for three days, and I had taken a slicing graze far down on my right thigh, probably from the single burst that little Aztec had gotten off my back our second day in the jungle. I stood. My eyes were glaring with anger, but Jack could not look me in the eye. He never could. Good thing, too. If the old saying 'if looks could kill' is true, Jack would have been a dead man right then and there.

I truly thought about pulling my .44 Mag and sending Jack straight to hell. But I held off that time. Nancy stalked out of the room and out of sight. As I caught up with her, she handed me a crumpled up restaurant napkin. As she walked away, I smoothed the paper and found a printed address followed by one word: Now.

Ten minutes later, my little Colt was parked behind a bright red Corvette and I was ringing the doorbell. The doorbell sound was a small, dainty chime that exactly fitted the petite figure and person of Nancy. The apartment was a mixture of comforting items. There was, she later told me, an Aubusson rug on the floor in front of a working fireplace. On a shelf, the bright lights of a scanner blinked, and I heard, "To our left, if you look down, you can see Lake Cumberland, one of Kentucky's many man-made lakes. We are approximately fourteen minutes from our destination."

"Hear that?" Nancy's voice came from the bedroom, where she had gone after letting me in. "Sounds like an airline captain punched the wrong button and is broadcasting what he meant to tell his passengers." I nodded. "Don't believe it," she answered. "That's not an airline frequency. That is a bug planted by our guys."

I thought it must have been one hell of a bug to reach Nancy's apartment. Then, I remembered it was probably something like thirty thousand feet, and at five and a half miles up, a 747 would make one hell of an antenna.

"What's the deal?" I asked, still a little uncomfortable in the unfamiliar surroundings. She came out of the bedroom dressed in a black exercise outfit that was a perfect contrast to her platinum hair and pale complexion.

"There was some suspicion that some captain was relaying a shipment of interstate cocaine. Supposed to be a new route cutting Lawrenceburg out of the relay."

"Lawrenceburg?"

"Yeah. A little fart of a town about twenty miles west of

Lexington. Anderson County, I think. Lots of old whiskey money now. There's a little factory or two and some rich farmers. Their big lick is the cocaine trade through Florida. Been going on for a least a generation.

"We'll probably hit them, maybe, one day," I stated. "They've got to have political protection to have stayed in business that long."

"Exactly." She nodded and went to a dry bar in the corner. "And how many politicians have we hit lately?" After a short pause, she continued. "That's right, unless you count that ridiculous little colonel in Guatemala. And he was an accident."

"Accident? Hell, he was trying to blow my damn head off! He was bound to get killed," I told her.

"Think back, Duncan. We've been through too much to be formal now. Think back to that little scenario. In your memory, how was the firefight spread?" I thought for a moment. The fighting had seemed spotty, above the sound of what was heard directly around Sean and me. And wherever there had been the deep chatter of an Ingram, there had been the snarl of M16s. Like the Unicorns were being singled out.

"They knew we were undercover ops," I told her. "They were more concerned with us than with what they took for locals."

"My whole point is they were waiting for you. What pot farmer just happens to have regular army hanging around carrying surface-to-air missiles on the very day a team is scheduled to destroy his crop? And don't forget those three days you and Sean spent in that jungle. Do you think they were going to mount a rescue operation? Hell's no!"

"Leaks happen," I told her. "And Jack and I are old friends. He wouldn't let information like that get out. I mean, he's a baboon's ass, but he isn't THAT stupid." But inside, those three days were really starting to bug me.

"You friend Jack is a greedy, scared, dirty piece of shit." She stated flatly, leaving no room for argument (Well, all right then! I thought). "You told me he was a stock boy in a supermarket before he joined the state police. You've seen him shoot. Does he show either confidence or competence?"

I had to laugh. Jack Hillard had himself made up for his lack of proficiency with firearms with proficiency of his mouth.

"He's manipulative," Nancy told me. "He gets other people to do the dirty work, just like that cold eel bastard Richards does. He's like a scout for a college basketball team. He worms around looking for people he can impress and recruit for Richards to coach. And whoever he works for, Richards is the coach."

"DEA," I put in automatically.

"So they say." Nancy didn't argue. "But I didn't ask you up here to argue alphabet soup. I noticed you at the briefing, and I liked the way you stayed with Sean and got him out of that trap. That proves to me you're loyal and responsible. Strong, too. Sean must weigh two twenty."

"Two thirty-five," I said, smiling.

"So," she handed me a glass tinted with the pale amber of Kentucky Bourbon. "I also saw you watching me and I bet you can't tell me three words Richards said," I could have, but I let her go on. "So you like the way I look. I like the way you look. Are you interested in breaking one of Richard's and Jack's rules?" I don't know what the look in my eyes was, but it must have been readable.

"I propose," she lifted her own glass, "That we become better acquainted. At this point, that's all. Don't ask, and don't push. We just let things develop as they suit us, okay?"

"Sure." I would have agreed to digital amputation to get to know this girl. No, not girl. Woman.

"Now." She turned businesslike. "I have something to show you." What she showed me was a newspaper clipping. It said: 'Colonel Mario de Vaca and fourteen of his troops have been killed in a rebel attack on the sugar plantation that was his country home. Ten rebels and three American mercenaries also died in the unsuccessful attack.'

"I'm sorry, Duncan," she said softly as I handed the scrap of paper back to her. "They were associates of yours, and although I'm not a native myself, I know how Kentuckians don't sleep well in a jungle grave." She handed me another clipping. This one told how seven U.S. Army soldiers and a three-man helicopter crew had disappeared on a training flight over the Pacific Ocean. Neither wreckage nor bodies had been recovered.

"Covering their ass," I said slowly.

"You got it ... Hammer," she replied, smiling.

Somehow, I had never really thought about how easy it is to account for the dead. As far as I had known, the dead had usually been on the other side. But I was learning fast. Damn fast.

The next time our little "crew" landed in that part of the world was just over six months later.

We were a seven man team. Well, six men and one woman. Hee, hee. We were staying on the bad side of Mexico City in a rundown hotel that gave roach hotels a good name. Our orders where simple. Stay put. Two would go out for food and drink twice a day and *only* twice a day. Stay put, and wait for orders.

Well, yeah, about that: After seven or eight days of this (I forget how many), we all decided to have a night out. Bad idea. We wound up in this dive bar that I swear looked like something like a bad movie. We all sat down and ordered drinks and things started out okay.

Things went to hell when a rather large and very drunk, uhm, Mexican gentleman asked Nancy to dance. After being nice and trying to avoid any trouble, trouble happened anyways. When Nancy stood up, I stood up with her. The rest of our crew pushed their chairs back so they could move quicker if needed.

Oh hells, was it needed!

You see, this "gentleman" had friends. Lots of friends.

I won't bore you with all the details. But, here's what happened. It was a fight. A big fight. A bad fight! Toward the end of this very quick fight, Nancy kicked one of the "friends" in the chest. So what? You ask. Well, she was wearing spiked heel boots. The spikes were covered with stainless steel, pretty much making them daggers. She buried that spiked heel in that man's chest. Right through the heart. I quickly looked for and found a knife on the bar and then plunged it into the wound already made by her heel.

"Get her and the rest of you out of here!" I screamed.

My plan, such as it was, was for me to take the rap for what had happened to the guy and I'll be damned if it didn't work! So, as you may well guess I was worked over *very* well by a dozen or so Mexican police and thrown into their jail. Now, it wasn't like Sean, Nancy and the others could just walk in, flash ID and out I walked. No, this had to be worked a tad differently.

About two days later, I was busted out. Yes, that's right, I was busted out! But during those two days I was having a staring contest with someone I called "Big Bubba." This guy was, I guessed, about three hundred plus pounds and just waiting for me to fall asleep (like *that* was gonna happen). Also, I had to go to the bathroom really bad and had no desire to use a bucket in the corner.

So I was sitting there and heard Morse code being tapped on the wall. I had no idea what it said, but I took the hint! A couple of minutes later the whole back side of the building was blown out. Sean stuck his head and shouted, "Hey Dunc, you need to move, we've got to go!"

Didn't have to tell me twice. I ran over Big Bubba, who had been knocked face down by the explosion, and I think I may have stepped on the back of his head as I ran.

Later, after meeting with officials from the U.S and Mexican governments it was agreed on that I was to *never* enter Mexico again. To do so would mean I could be shot on sight.

Hey, no problem.

C H A P T E R 13

I woke with a faint feeling of regret about my wife's long-standing rejection of my sexual needs, and a great feeling of satisfaction with Nancy. Here was the woman I should have married, and might yet. Our advantage was each other's complete realization of how the other thought. From the beginning, Frieda's first, last and middle thought was "Gimme!"

You still meet that kind, up in the hills. Usually they're inclined to religion, Baptist religion. Inclined to use religion, that is. Get a hand on her thigh and she says, "You'll have to marry me first." After she has picked out her man, though, if she has judged him right, she'll let him have the feel with the warning. Then, later, she will let him have what both want and then sigh, "Now you'll have to marry me."

Sometimes, like in my case, the boy is young enough or idealistic enough to go along with what she wants. Then, half the time she will turn from an untouchable saint to an insatiable slut who will spread her legs for anybody but her husband — well, sometimes for him. I suspect that's in case somebody else's seed sprouts.

You know, what makes this even more ironic ... or hell, pathetic, is that Frieda wasn't even Kentucky born and raised. Nope. Ohio. Columbus, actually.

Nancy Cramer, on the other hand, once she made up her mind, was more the "take me" kind. Remember when you were a kid and it came time to choose sides for a team sport or game? Of course you do. Don't lie! If you were ever the team captain you know the look the kid gets on his face when he's eager to be on your team and pleads, "Take me!" That look is something of pleading and something of fear of being left out of the fun. That look is exactly the same as the one Nancy would get, except it was accompanied by the dewy-eyed assurance of acceptance and mutual pleasure.

There were times when we stepped into the shower and just held each other while the water purified us. Sometimes storm and dust was washed away. Sometimes it was storm, dust, and blood. And sometimes we stepped out of the shower and walked straight to the bed without the benefit of towels. Those times we would just lie there, holding each other and telling ourselves our wet skin was what made us shiver.

"Duncan," she finally asked me, "What are you going to do about Frieda? I'm not pressuring you, or asking you for anything. It's just that you're not happy and you come in jumpy. I don't mind if you work your tensions out on me, 'cause I know it's not a game with us. Hell, you're pretty damn good at making my tensions go away, too. I don't care about her, and I don't think I'll care about any others you'll have. I didn't exactly save my cherry for you, you know."

I had known that without even thinking about it. I guess that shows how important the matter was to me. After she flew me out of that trap in Central America, it just seemed like we had claims on each other. I reached a hand up to stroke her left breast. Just an intimate caress, the kind not meant to lead to anything more. She tilted her head so her hair covered my hand like a veil.

The truth was, I didn't want to think about ending my marriage to Frieda. After all, she was my second wife and I wasn't even twenty-four yet. I knew it had to happen; I just didn't want to think about it. Anger was all I felt every time I thought of that marriage. So I changed the subject.

"The question is, what are old Jack and Richards going to do about *us*?" I said. "You know we're in direct opposition of their 'no fraternizing' rule."

Suddenly she was grave, not just serious as she had been before, but actually grave.

"Please, let's not talk about either of those two. They scare me.

Jack is so full of himself he thinks everything that opens up instead of hanging down is available to him and should by God love him."

"You know what Sean would say," I teased her, but she interrupted me.

"Yes, I know. He would cite two or three authorities to indicate Jack has to prove he's a man and interested in women. Then he would cite more, to question the first two or three. They really do scare me. He and Richards both. Jack is so gung-ho. He reminds me of a Boy Scout leader my older brother used to have, all panting and eager to do whatever is scheduled, whether it's tying knots or carving animals out of soap or wood.

"Course that was before they found out he was a pervert, but that's for when we need a good laugh. Not now. Then there's Richards. I swear sometimes I think he's not even alive. And I wonder who he works for."

"DEA," I said automatically.

"Really?" She was still grave. "Did anyone ever say that? I'm serious now. Does he work for the feds or the state? CIA, FBI … Mafia? He never shows any emotion. I think the only things he likes are those cheap cigars and his Hershey bars, though how he bears to mix the two flavors is more than I can imagine."

"Maybe they go together like peanut butter and chocolate," I tried to joke, and she turned those deep blue eyes on me with a slightly reproving look.

Ahh, shit, I thought.

"His eating habits may be amusing," she said, "But he certainly isn't. I tell you, I can't believe he's human sometimes. Where does he live? Does he have a life outside of briefing and debriefing? Is he military? Sometimes he acts like it. Or is he some super-secret branch nobody's ever heard of? Or is Sean right? Is he our Ernst Kaltenbrunner?"

"Kaltenbrunner?" I asked. It occurred to me that I had never asked Sean who Ernst was.

"The Gestapo chief," she answered. "The Nazi secret police. Though with his body type he looks more like an elongated Dr. Goebbels."

That statement, made my blood run cold, though I knew not why ... then.

"Do you think that's who we are?" I would have to turn that one over later. "A secret police?"

"Of course we are. Death squads can't function without some official protection. You see, that's what worries me. We don't know who we're working for. Oh, I know we were taken to the Federal Building in Lexington and sworn in, and we get most of our orders from Jack and his asswipes, but what if the direction of the whole operation was turned over to Jack and Richards? Do you not find that to be a scary fucking thought?" I had to chew on that one for a while. I decided that was a pretty frightening thought.

Gestapo.

For us, worse than Gestapo, for we had no official standing. If the squad didn't exist, what of us? Did we exist? I wondered how many Unicorns had been tucked into unmarked graves in the hills. Just what did Jack think he was buying for his thousand dollars a week in used bills? I knew what Richards thought he was buying. He was like that character Sean had told me about, the one who pays well but always takes the soul for his pay. Some German wrote a play about him, called him Mephistopheles.

I guess that made Hillard, Jack Allen Hillard, his imp. Start it with a "p" and it becomes even shabbier. Nancy was becoming as bad as Sean about making me think. All at once, I was Wyatt Earp risking life and limb to clean up the country. If Albert Richards was our Ernst Kaltenbrunner, I was just some shitty stick used to stir up the outhouse that was the business-politics-religion-Mafia square of Eastern Kentucky.

Lions, tigers and bears, oh fuck.

"Next week," Nancy pressed my hand to her bosom, just over her heart, "You'll be operating in some place like Nicaragua, and there will be records to prove that you've been there for weeks. Probably training the Contras in unarmed defense." I twisted away from her so suddenly she winced in pain as I bruised her breast.

"You know something, don't you?"

"Of course. I wasn't going to tell you, but Jack's been trying to screw me for about as long as I've been on the team."

"Why, that slimy bastard!" I was really pissed. "That son of a bitch is married!" That got us both laughing and eased the tension that had boiled up. She put her forefinger on my nose and pushed.

"He married into coal money on one side and into politics on the other. That little wife of his, the one that you tried so hard to get into the hay with, happens to be the niece — the favorite niece, if the only legitimate niece — of Dick Haley, our local circuit judge, and a good friend of your father's."

"Hey!" I laughed. "I was just a teenager. And how did you know about that?"

"I have my ways," she laughed right back at me. "Now she might have screwed you," she continued on, "And still might. But she's one of those big dogs. She couldn't have married you. You're like me, an outsider. One of the little people, good for a recreational or therapeutic roll in the hay. But there would be no profit in marrying you."

I'd known about Glenda Maupin being Judge Dick Haley's niece. Everybody in Eastern Kentucky knows who everybody else is kin to. Most of them can tell you who the real father of the kid is, no matter whom the mother is married to. What I knew, but Nancy didn't, was that Glenda Maupin's real father was quietly reported to not be her lawful father, Clarence Maupin of coal wealth, but Maupin's half brother, Richard Haley, who was renowned to have somehow amassed a rival fortune out of his judgeship.

In Kentucky, judges are expected to get rich, just as commonwealth attorneys, so nobody really complains. If somebody gets away with something — let's say murder — it's assumed that he paid someone off. The crime itself is usually secondary in interest to what it cost him to get out of it. There is an assumption that the victim is guilty — at least of getting caught — and that justice of some sort is served.

A direct payoff to a judge saves all the paperwork of giving jacked up contracts to the politician's friends. These judges are actually admired in Kentucky, as everywhere else. Another way that judges, commonwealth attorneys, local law enforcement and their underlings get rich in Kentucky is to get into the pawn shop, loan company and finance companies. Big money there. Dangerous money. And believe you me, they'll fight, murder, and lock up anyone they have to in order to protect it.

Believe me, I know.

I found out the hard way (next book, I promise).

CHAPTER 14

Before she pointed the red Corvette west, Nancy had given me the number of her brother in California. She called me on Tuesday, the day she arrived there, and told me she felt great, both about her vacation and her condition. She teased me a little, and then said it was great to be with her brother again. She had told him about us, and about my impending divorce. She must have chatted for an hour, and that made me feel better than I had felt for weeks.

This was going to be my third marriage, and I had a feeling this one would be the good one. In the real world, Nancy's flight attendant job combined with my schools ought to put us well into the six-figure income bracket. We hung up the phone after exchanging I love yous and take cares. Then I realized I hadn't mentioned I wanted to marry her.

To this day, I can't remember whether I was assuming she already knew that, or whether I was honoring her wish to have time to think. Time to think. That is generally a misnomer. What we really need is the time to relive our emotional experiences and see if we can live with them.

From the time I saw that piece of transportation equipment walk into the briefing room nearly a year ago, I had wanted her. When I was half-dead with exhaustion from carrying Sean and bleeding from wounds I didn't even know I had, when that chopper first whooped-whooped into the jungle, my first thoughts were about that long platinum hair, and that walk.

For the rest of the day I was euphoric. Everything was coming together for me. A bad marriage was coming to an end, and the one woman I loved wasn't concerned about what she had come to call my letdown liaisons, as Sean had named my follow-up fucks.

I closed the school early and finished the last of my business before leaving for home. I negotiated the twenty yards to my Colt and headed in the direction of Inez. I pulled to the curb behind a gray Cadillac Seville. I swung my legs out of the Colt and pulled myself to my feet. As usual, my street footwear was sneakers and my grip on the stair rail made my progress quiet and steady, though I began to hear a pulsing beat as I neared the top of the stairs. I guessed it sounded something like bedsprings.

When Frieda had whined about my waking her up as I came home late, I had cleaned and oiled the front door hinges and lock. They were absolutely silent once the key was in place. I skirted the coffee table and the pulsing beat picked up speed. The short hallway was carpeted and my weaving footfalls were silent, at least to my ears. The lock hinge on the bedroom door was as silent as the entry door. Then I pushed the door open and hit the light switch.

As I did so, Frieda moaned and Doctor French, her dentist, arched his hips for a final thrust between her thighs. He got his gun about the same time I pulled mine from its holster. I had seen that same triumphant look on the face of the prick I had shot in the farmhouse after he had stabbed the little girl in the neck. William Howard French's look changed the same way the punk bastard's had when he saw the big .44 Magnum come out from under my jacket.

Frieda screamed, "You goddamn son of a bitch!" as I took aim at the dentist's slender bare ass. I blew apart an ugly lamp her mother had given us as a wedding gift. A grotesque bust of Elvis Presley.

"Elvis has *left* the building!" I shouted. I was sorry to miss Dr. French's ass, but overjoyed to see the lamp with its asswipe face dissolve into shreds some archaeologist might puke with joy over ten thousand years from now.

My second shot blew the footboard of the bed apart, and my third hit the nightstand. I was surprised to see Trojans flying around the room like Hector around the walls of Troy. I think I giggled then.

I had never used a rubber in my life.

By now the dentist was off my wife and sniveling in one corner of my bedroom. He was standing straddle-legged and my sense of humor was coming back. I aimed a foot below his balls and fired two rounds. The little bastard surprised me by shrieking and charging at me with his pale hands hooked into claws.

Please understand. I didn't give a rat's ass about her with this guy. But come on! Get a freaking hotel room! Not in *my* bed!

I had to admire the little son of a bitch. He was doing exactly what I would have done. Only I would have done it sooner with anything that could possibly be used as a weapon. As I said, my sense of humor was coming back, and I snapped my last round off into the floor between us before tossing the Magnum into a chair piled with a neatly folded three-piece suit.

I pulled the 35mm camera I always carried with me from inside my jacket pocket. Then I snapped the last five or six shots on the roll, trying to catch Frieda's wet belly in the background of the charging naked dentist. I dropped the camera and caught the dentist by the throat. His flaccid dick had shrunk to about the size of one of the rounds for my .44 Magnum, an unfired round though, to give him credit. The little fornicator must have weighed all of a hundred fifty pounds drained (I know, I laughed too), so I lifted his two feet off the floor and flicked him back on the bed. He landed between my wife's knees and I swear she clamped them shut.

"Go for it, big boy," I told him, and promised myself I would spread the word that he was hung like an unfired .44 Magnum round. I picked up one of the undamaged Trojans, tore open the foil wrap, and tossed it between them. It landed between Frieda's breasts and I had to laugh again. "Go for it," I told them again, "If you still got it in you."

Then just for the hell of it, I tore open another one, blew it up and let the air out so it made that funny sound a balloon makes when it slips out of your grasp when trying to blow it up.

Frieda hissed, "Bastard!" as I closed the door behind me. But she was reaching for the dentist's little ass as she said it. I had picked up my .44 Mag and camera as I was walking out the bedroom door.

Out of pure instinct, I reloaded my weapon and got a new roll of film from the top of the refrigerator, reloading the camera as well. The used film I placed in my pocket; the camera I tossed on the kitchen table.

I staggered back down the stairs feeling overjoyed, laughing my as off and calculating how long it would take me to drive the mile and a half back to my school. I laughed out loud with delight as I thought of the dentist's lean ass sandwiched between Frieda's well-padded thighs.

By the next morning, word was out I had tried to shoot my wife, which was a lie. I hadn't aimed a single shot at her. I hadn't even tried to aim at a vital part of Dr. French. After eleven I drove down to Dad's office and was met by a wry grin.

"Didn't really try to hurt them, did you?" he asked.

"I don't know." I grinned back. "I wasn't there."

"Well, Frieda says she's not going to have you arrested," he told me, as he rolled his eyes. "She was here just now looking all weepy and innocent and telling me you came in drunk and wanted to take indecent pictures of her, which she, as a good Christian, refused. She brought back your camera, but she had taken the film out and exposed it. You shouldn't have shot up the place with hardball."

"Only every other round," I told him. "I always alternate soft nose and hardball." The hardball full metal jacketed bullet in the .44 Magnum is a car-killer, I know from experience.

"Well, I've been down and looked the damage over. Worst thing I saw was that you blew a wall stud apart that pushed through the outer wall a quarter mile away and killed   a propane tank of the Genovies'. Took the fire department most of the night to keep it from spreading and put the damn thing out. "You hot load those damn things?" Dad asked.

All I could do was smile.

I felt the roll of film in my pocket, the roll I wasn't about to hand over to Jack Hillard for developing.

"She'll file for divorce before the day is out," Dad went on. "I'd let her go. And son, remember this. This is Frieda we're talking about. I personally believe she'll swear out a warrant. Just be ready for it."

"I haven't had her for some time." I poured myself coffee from Dad's pot. "I'm running up to Lexington to get some film developed. And if she wants to do the warrant thing, more power to her." I turned back as I was opening the door, a horrible look on my face.

"Dad," I asked, "when are you ever gonna learn how to make a good cup of coffee?"

"Get the hell out of here," he laughed, as he threw the morning paper at me. I laughed back, and was on my way to Lexington.

I started remembering how Frieda was looking at me the night before. She would look at me, look at her dentist. Look at him, look at me, and on and on. I suddenly remembered something that happened when I was about eleven years old.

At that time we lived in a house that was right on the highway. No shit. You could stand on the front porch and spit onto the road. Well I could, anyways. I had a dog back then. A half Collie and half mutt. Kind of like most of the people around there, now that I think about it. Anyways, the day before a group of relatives had come for a visit. One of the kids, about my age, brought with him a bag of balloons.

Well Lucky, that was my dog's name, wanted those balloons. He jumped on this kid, knocking them from his hands. Lucky then proceeded to eat over half of the damn things! I kid you not, he just licked them up and swallowed. I went on with my kid's day never thinking much more about it.

Until the next morning.

Around seven a.m. or so, I heard Lucky running and yelping in the front yard. I walked out, and all I could do was sit on the edge of the front porch and watch. One of the balloons Lucky had swallowed was sticking out of his ass about six inches. This poor dog was running and stopping. Thing was, every time he stopped running, he farted. This dog's farts were blowing up that balloon!

So there I sat, watching Lucky run from left to right, right to left and farting that balloon up. I felt like I was watching a tennis match. After about forty-five minutes or so, that balloon was big enough to pop. And it did! Lucky let out a doggie scream and started running down the highway. I guess Lucky wasn't so "Lucky" after all. Just like Frieda and her dentist.

CHAPTER 15

The next morning, the bitch — I mean, Frieda — was gone. Her dentist too, was gone. As a matter of fact, he left Inez that night and I never saw him again. The gossip says that he took a teaching position at the University of Kentucky, but we all know how that goes. His wife stayed around town for a few months. But she was a dowdy sort who looked almost grandmotherly at thirty-two and finally left town with some sort of religious nut cluster.

Anyway, Frieda ran to the judge who was some kind of kissing, if not fucking, cousin, and he signed a warrant for my arrest on charges of wanton endangerment. Kentucky law is a sort of shit-on-a-brick setup. It used to be any citizen could go to a magistrate with fifty cents and swear out a warrant for anybody. Not anymore. That was too democratic. Under the new laws the commonwealth attorney decides what warrants are issued. He can refuse to issue a warrant, say, in a sniping case where a perpetrator is caught with the rifle in his hand, because the victim did not see him fire a shot. Even if the warrant was issued, you are not sure of an arrest. The executive branch, sheriff, or chief of police may misplace, lose or simply refuse to serve the warrant.

Dad simply used this pocket veto and after all, this *was* inside city limits. Then Jack found work for me outside the state. I was emotionally up enough to look forward to this assignment. Besides, I needed the money to pay for the damage my .44 Mag had done to the apartment, and, though I tried to forget it, the Genovies' restaurant. I did get one of those midnight warning calls from

Richards. "Either quiet the problem, or eliminate the problem," I was ordered. Eliminate that fat ass? What did he think I was, a miracle worker? It would have taken a black hole to hide that ass.

As it was, I spent more than half a week stashed in a hotel, waiting. Waiting and fuming. Did I say waiting? I was glad Frieda was gone. Her lack of interest in sex with me had long ago freed whatever inhibitions I might have had about looking for love elsewhere and taking it wherever I found it. The after-action orgasms didn't count as love. But I didn't find any that week. Actually, I didn't even look. I couldn't even get Nancy on the phone and was pissed till I remembered this was the week she was driving in a stockcar race in Los Angeles. That girl was just as good in a racecar as she was in a chopper.

I loafed around a local gym, and then began reading a lot, one of the things I always kill time with. I waited so long I began to recognize some of the local drug dealers and became so bored I was considering beginning a freelance operation. After all, Jack, the DEA, the Mafia, or somebody was paying me a thousand dollars a week to control drug movement. In the end though, I just made mental notes that I later wrote down and forwarded to Richards through Jack. I was lonely, bored, frustrated and horny by the end of the second week. I was also two thousand dollars richer, at least in accounts receivable.

At about midnight on the second Friday, the call came from Jack. We were to run surveillance on an isolated warehouse in Camden County along the Georgia shoreline border. The plan was that I would go alone with binoculars, night scope, infrared camera, micro-recorder, etc. You know, all that crap I didn't want or need. I would also have my usual Ingram and .45 plus ammunition. It made a comfortable load in my backpack. I also had the backup of Sean and two other Unicorns in case something went wrong.

I killed two men that night. Remember, what your government pays you to do makes it all right. I set up my observation post atop a neighboring building that gave me access to the sights and sounds coming from the warehouse operation. You have to realize that some of these people, maybe most of them in some cases, are ex-military. Despite the contempt for authority, the army teaches all but the primitive patriot and among the skills they learn is how to secure a perimeter.

Now without bragging, I am good at what I do. I can slink, sneak, and fade with the best of them. At the time I was the best our side had. The other side had someone better. As I said before, I killed two men and settled back, taping sounds and photographing through an open window of the warehouse-factory operation. The only sound I heard from the guy was a slight rush of air from the blackjack as it came down on the back of my head. There was no flash of excruciating pain. No time to try and jerk away. Just a sudden blank space in my memory that I knew about only when I came to (but, after many years to reflect, I believe it was something else, much farther away than a man with a blackjack).

When I did come to, I wished I hadn't. My arms were trussed together over my head and there were what felt like several tons of cord around my ankles. My chin was covered with dried blood and about three of my teeth were loose. Blood was dripping off my left heel from what I later learned was a deep scrape on my calf. I also had the headache from hell and I could feel the swelling at the back of my head. I figured out that I had been worked over pretty good. I also knew from the pain in my wrist and muscles that I was suspended from a ceiling beam.

When I opened my puffy eyelids, I was looking at who I assumed was my captor, and he stared back with slightly pursed lips. He had my muscle tone spread over a slightly broader frame. He was clean-shaven and wore his long hair in a ponytail. When he saw me looking at him, he casually backhanded me across the nose and mouth. My nose started dripping again.

"Who are you?" he asked in an accent I could never identify.

"Who do you work for?" The hand slapped back and forth across my face with each question. "DEA?" Slap. "FBI?" Slap. "CIA?" Slap. "IRS?" He went on through every institutional agency he could think of (and some I had never heard of). Then he got tired of slapping and began to use me as a punching bag. That sent me swinging in the air. Then he grabbed me and turned me 'round and 'round like a kid winding up the rope on a tree swing. When he let go, I unwound and he aimed random punches at me. Eventually he got tired of getting no for an answer and started working on my head again. I passed out.

I awoke, sopping wet from the water they had splashed over me, and the beatings started again, this time with a difference. My captor conferred with some others in that peculiar accent of his. Then he picked up what I recognized as my knife and walked toward me, thumbing the edge. He seemed satisfied when the edge curled skin from his thumb. Then he placed the tip at my navel and let it travel on its own weight down to the base of my penis. At that point, as I felt the blood well into the shallow trench the knife made, he suddenly pivoted and drove the blade deep into my left thigh.

The stoicism learned in the logging camps stood me in good play. When an ax slips or bounces and bites flesh, you don't rant or scream, you endure. A rolling log crushes a foot, you endure. A felled tree gets a mind of its own and sways with the wind and you find yourself pinned, you endure.

"Tough one, ain't he?" Came from outside of my field of vision. "He'll soften up," came in that particular soft accent, as the knife was twisted in the wound. Fresh blood began to gush onto the floor. There is one thing about pain. Its repetition can send the conscious mind on vacation. I don't know how many times that happened to me while I was hanging there. I don't even know how long I was hanging there. I do have some vague notion of being lifted down and then lifted back up, along with the memories of beating and drenching and soiling myself.

Eventually, my system was empty and the back of my throat felt like I had been breathing sand. I decided my two choices were to die or pray for the cavalry to charge in. With my Indian blood, I couldn't be too sure which side the cavalry would be on. I decided to pull an old Indian trick of deciding to die, and I promptly did, superficially.

No, I will not tell everything that happened to me that night. Some things are better left buried. But I will tell you; I didn't know what I was in for. The foreign prick who had been torturing me hit on a new method of bringing me to. Instead of risking splashing himself with water, he just reached both hands up to my side and snapped one of my floating ribs. That brought me back to the present in a snap, literally.

Between the beatings and awakenings, I later found I had a total of six broken ribs, and was having one hell of a time trying to die. It looked like they were trying to kill me before I could die on my own.

"Talk, tough man," my captor said. "Talk and we will let you go. The shipment's long been delivered and disbanded. You have nothing to gain but more pain."

"I work," I began through cracked lips and loosened teeth, "for Archie Bunker."

"Who's this Bunker?"

"A fucking TV show," came from the background. The gloved fist with its hands of leather landed on the side of my head and I was out once more.

CHAPTER 16

When I drifted back into consciousness, the group in the room was looking relaxed, bored, and curious. What looked like a truck driver wearing a bad suit had wandered in and stood looking up at me with a bemused expression as he smoked his cigar.

"So this is your prize," he said. "He looks like owl-shit." He touched the burning tip of the cigar to the stab wound in my leg and I drew a breath to scream. I knew I'd had enough. But life imitates art and sometimes imitates the movies. My first hint that the cavalry had arrived was when the man with the cigar held the bloodied butt up to examine it. At the beginning of one second, he was staring at it as if in love with it. At the end of that same second, he started to scream as he stared at the bloody stump where the forty-five slug had amputated his hand at the wrist. It was a ragged job.

Two more rounds took him in the head and body and flung him out of my sight as the rest of the cavalry went into action. There is no other way to describe the events in the warehouse — it was a massacre. The authoritative rumble of MAC-10s was overlaid by the snarling statements of Uzis and M16s. Forty-fives played counterpoint to thirty-eights, and once, in a corner behind stacked crates, there was the unmistakable flash and roar of a grenade. At this sound, the civilians hesitated in their firing, but the Unicorns went right on about their work.

Let me tell you, it gives you a funny feeling to be hanging from a rope with fire in your insides and watching men die around you like cockroaches in a Raid commercial. If men were there, they died. As for me, I was still hanging from this fucking beam and trying to shrug my shoulders enough to set my body turning so I could see more. My enemies were dying, and I could have no part in the killing of the bastards. That hurt me worse at that moment then my broken ribs and hands, bleeding leg, and bleeding asshole.

When the warehouse was secured, Jack trotted over and stood looking up at me. I was somehow surprised to see his little snub thirty-eight smoking in his hand. If I had been in less pain I might have laughed and said, "Archie Bunker, I presume." As it was, I wondered if any of the bodies on the floor had thirty-eight slugs in them. If they did, I wanted to grab a forty-five and make sure they were completely dead.

Sean walked up, dangling a warm smelling Colt .45 from his right forefinger. He raised a hand to Jack's shoulder and roughly pushed him aside. He just glanced at me and at the rope before reaching up and gripping me under the armpits to lift me up, to bring the strain off my arms. Then he nodded toward the sheathed knife on his hip to another Unicorn with black face paint and ordered him to cut.

As Sean laid me on my side I heard Jack say, "Get a medic in here." Somebody, presumably Army, was listening on the other end of the handheld radio that had chocolate stains on its bottom.

Sean took his knife and made short work of my bonds, then began chafing my wrists. My hands were numb and swollen. The rest of the squad gathered around me. Somebody brought a Navy-issue blanket and wrapped it around me, while somebody else thought to pour water into my mouth.

Nobody thought about what was most on my mind. Nobody offered me a gun. When I could open and close my right hand, I reached for the forty-five Sean had holstered. "What, lad?" Sean asked.

"Ponytail," I managed to croak, and Jack glanced at me quickly. Sean wrinkled his brow, but handed me the pistol. I knew he had automatically put in a fresh magazine. When I tried to stand up, the pain in my legs matched that in my arms and ass. With Sean's help I managed to stagger to my feet and make a tour of the warehouse. I did not count bodies, or body parts, but they easily outnumbered the Unicorns. The only one I couldn't make out at first glance was the one who had taken the grenade. I did finally find part of his head, and he had a red beard.

By the time I had satisfied myself that Ponytail was not among the Unicorn's victims, a helicopter had landed on the warehouse parking lot and men with a stretcher had come to carry me away. I was almost wishing the chopper had been a hearse.

Ponytail had gotten away, and the Unicorns had faded away toward debriefing. Men in the uniform of Georgia state police soft-footed through the blood, body parts, and all the spent cartridge cases, photographing and shaking their heads as I was carried out. The injection I received must have been morphine, because before the chopper touched down at the airport or Army base or whatever the hell it was, I was out as if Ponytail had clubbed me again.

When I came to, I struggled to sit up but found I was strapped securely down. It would be days before I was lucid enough to know that they had flown me to Fort Knox to have me attended to at the base hospital.

A month later I was released from the hospital, and found good old Inez pretty much the same as when I had left. Same asswipe people still in political office. A cover story had gone out long before I returned. My asinine assistant instructors had damned near put me out of business. That could be fixed. My ribs were just about healed, but I was more out of shape than I had ever been in. I had undergone reconstruction of my lower colon and repeated hemorrhoid surgery. The doctors recommended I take it easy for at least the next few months. I figured they were used to dealing with regular Army guys who are notoriously hard to cure of anything that can keep them off the active duty list.

I went back to my regular schedule as much as I could. Another emotion I was feeling was hate. Hate for a clean-shaven ponytailed son of a bitch who was a dead man if our paths ever crossed again on any part of the globe, whether it be a drug bust or a consular function.

And if you can read English, Ponytail, read this: I know you are out there and I suspect you have either high-placed friends or diplomatic immunity. But no son of a bitch is immune to a knife or sword to the throat or a quick twist of the garrote. And not even presidents are immune to a well-placed bullet of a competent marksman. If we ever meet again, you son of a bitch, your ass is mine.

CHAPTER 17

I debated calling Nancy when I got home that night. With the time difference, it wouldn't have been much past dusk there, but I decided against it. I got six hours of sleep and did my four-mile run before breakfast, despite the red sunrise. "Red sky at morning, sailors take warning." I remembered the weather rhyme, and it became a silent chant with my footfalls. But there are few sailing opportunities in eastern Kentucky, and I found myself changing the chant to "runners take warning." The chant got into my head and bothered me as the red light intensified. "Take warning, take warning," till I was snapped back to reality by the blow of a diesel horn and looked up to see a coal truck bearing down on me, forcing me to jog up the middle of Wickerfield Road.

I went home to shower and change, and, I must say, the house never looked better. No more Frieda, and no more of Frieda's shit. All of her Elvis memorabilia crap was gone. Thank God! Hallelujah! The phrase "Free at last, free at last, thank God Almighty, I'm free at last," came bursting into my mind. After a good, long, hot shower I drove down to Dad's office. I could hear the screaming from the street, so I walked slowly up to the door and opened it just enough to get a peek inside.

There stood my father, the police chief of Inez, Kentucky, standing behind his desk with some papers in his hand, waving them around everywhere. One of his third shift officers was standing in front of him.

"Just what the hell did you think you were doing?" He shouted, his brogue about the thickest I had ever heard it. "I don't give a rat's ass *who* he is! Duncan, get you arse in here!" He yelled at me.

Only one thought came to my mind right then. How in the hell did he know it was me standing beside the corner of the door? Go in, you betcha I went in.

"Duncan, we would like, if you please, your opinion on something."

"Sure, Dad," was all I could think to say.

"Officer Bill Spence here, last night, pulled Judge Dick Haley over in a traffic stop last night." This sounds good, I thought. "Judge Haley was drunk and disorderly, and to top it off he had an underage prostitute in the car with him!" I couldn't help myself. I started laughing so hard tears began to flow.

"Well, your opinion, Duncan, if you please." Dad wasn't fazed by my laughing.

"Ah, yes, well," I started as I choked back the laughter. "I have a question for Officer Spence first, before I give my opinion."

"Go ahead. Ask away," Dad said.

"How much did the great Judge Haley give you to let him go?" I asked.

Officer Spence looked like he had just swallowed a turd.

"A hundred dollars," he said, though it came out more like a squawk. I thought my father would die.

"You stupid fucking asshole!" he screamed.

"Chief, sir, it will never happen again." Officer Spence could barely get the words out.

"Oh, you got that right, boy. As of right now you got ten days suspension. Ten days for me to cool off. Now get the hell out of my sight!" With that said, Officer Spence, tail between his legs, almost ran out of the office.

"Hey, Dad, I thought you wanted my opinion." I said, smiling from ear to ear.

"Shut up and let's go get some breakfast," he retorted, a smile on his face.

We walked across the street to the famous Inez Café, known state-wide for its "under the table" illegal deals. But the food wasn't bad, and the two of us together ate a good helping of steak, eggs, potatoes, and drank about a gallon of black coffee. After the meal was over, we engaged in some small talk when Dad finally looked me straight in the eye.

"How are you doing, son?" he asked with all his fatherly know-how.

"I'm doing fine, Dad," I finally said.

"Look, Duncan, I know a little about what happened to you. Don't ask me how I know, let's just say I know. So, how are you really?"

I sat there for at least a full minute before answering. I gazed around the restaurant for a moment, noting the hard, hateful looks we were getting from some of Inez's great legal minds. I turned my eyes back to my father.

"You know Dad, I think that I'm really doing good," I said, with a slight grin on my face.

What I wanted to say was, I am so fucked up right now, all I want to do is blow my brains out! But did I say that? Oh hell's no.

"Listen, son, if you ever want to talk, or just go fishing or something, I'm here, OK?" he told me. Those words meant a lot to me right then.

"I'll hold you to that, Dad," I said.

"Good," was all he said back. Then he looked at his watch. "Time to make rounds around the great city of Inez. Want to come along?" he asked me.

"Can't today, Dad, I got business to tend to."

"Well, stay out of trouble," he said, dropping a hand on my shoulder. With that, he was out the door, leaving me to pick up the check! Good old Dad.

I checked in with the local bank about the land I wanted to expand into and then drove over to Paintsville at mid-noon. My day was coasting along euphorically when Jack's call came. As of now, he told me, I was on call for an in-country but out of state operation.

"There may be a little delay," he continued. "We got to get a new pilot. Our old one just got herself totaled in one of those famous California freeway pileups. When it's set we'll let you know."

He was gone and his last words transmitted themselves: No! No! No! My world was coming apart in an instant. "Red sky at morning, forever take warning." My heart was an aching void. Suddenly I was the sole survivor of what in a few months would have been a family with some meaning.

The jigsaw puzzle of my life had been ready to fall into place, the outer border, at least, had become connected and now all the corners were missing. I stood up, wheeled, and drove my fist through both sides of the wall separating my office from the gym. Then I got out the kit bag kept close by and dug out the short-barreled .44 Magnum I always carried. I do not know how long I sat there looking down the barrel of that awesome weapon two inches from my forehead, but finally the words, No, this is not the answer came into my head.

But the anger had to go, some way. I walked into the gym proper and looked at one of the big heavy canvas punching bags. I knew what I had to do, so I checked the time and dragged Nancy's brother's phone number out of my wallet. I sat down at my desk, wiping away tears as I dialed the number. Finally, after about half an hour, Simon Cramer and I had our one and only conversation.

"Listen Duncan," he told me. "I knew about you and Nancy, not that it matters now. What does matter is that I don't accept the police report. If a tanker truck blew a tire, she would have driven around it or through the flames. That girl could outdrive Andretti, and those trucks don't use second-rate tires, not out here. I'm just not satisfied with the police version. So these other people died. You know anyone is expendable in the circles you both move in. I still have connections in military intelligence who owe me some favors and I'm asking them to take a look, if they can get at the wreckage. It's too coincidental that both state cops who investigated the wreck to have been Kentucky born guys named Ross and Middleton."

I suppose I just moaned miserable at him. It was really a duty call, and I can't recall a single thing I said except "I loved her," and he responded, "I know she loved you. She was carrying the proof."

The conversation petered out with promises to keep in touch and I hung up the phone. Too many pieces seemed to be from another puzzle. Show me a problem and I will get through it to a simple, physical solution — direct action. Sean was, and Nancy had been, the thinkers among the Unicorns. Not the planners, but the questioners. The plans had come from Richards and through Jack, and God only knows what Richards based his planning on.

The next piece of the puzzle was slipped under my door at work, and it came four days later. It was a small square of newspaper that was undated and unsigned:

Four Die in Los Angeles Camper Explosion

```
    A man, his fiancée and his two
children died this afternoon in an
explosion in a motor home. Simon
Cramer, 34; Gloria Cramer, 4; Andrew
Cramer, 7; and Jodie Glazier, 26,
perished when their motor home
exploded and caught fire. The bodies
were burned beyond recognition.
    Sergeant Ross of the California
Highway Patrol theorized that a leaky
propane tank had touched off the
explosion.
```

It would be a long time before I could look at another woman without thinking of those eyes, that laugh, that walk. But life must go on.

CHAPTER 18

And life went on.

My next assignment, several weeks after Nancy's death, was an Ohio raid that turned out to be a bust. Not a raid, not a killing, not an arrest (not that we ever arrested anyone), just a plain clusterfuck.

The crop of pot on the highway right-of-way outside Athens had been removed by the roots and the ground harrowed over. Sean picked up a handful of soil and rubbed it in his palm.

"Rye grass."

He pointed to some slender seeds a quarter-inch long.

"Annual rye. Comes a rain, you'll have a quick cover crop here, at least for the summer."

He reached into the pocket of his black jacket and produced photos we had seen before. There was no doubt we had the right place. The curve of the right-of-way and the outcropping of gray stones proved that. The only thing missing was the lush growth of the shoulder-high marijuana plants that this photo showed us. I swore. I was thinking we might not get paid for the raid, or the non-raid.

"Calm down now, lad," Sean coaxed. "What's a quarter-ton of hash to us? This little stretch of highway right-of-way that didn't get mowed — that's forty by eighty feet? Only about six hundred thousand dollars on the street."

That was in the days before the Casey County growers started holding out for two hundred and fifty bucks an ounce and got Texas and Arkansas competition flying it at nine hundred bucks a pound. Sean snapped a few thirty-five millimeter shots of the site, being careful to get the rock outcropping in the pictures as we walked back to our transport — a double seated International pickup, its crew cab loaded with Unicorns, its bed holding gear under canvas.

"That it?" the voice of Unicorn David Anderson asked from inside.

Of all the Unicorns, I think I disliked David the most. Just one of those things. Too much of a pussy to be a killer. To be a Unicorn.

"Was," Sean answered. "We've measured it from all checkpoints, down to the tenth mile. That's the garden and the totems that've been dug."

Another voice said, "Shit! And we're missing the demolition derby."

"And the water polo competition," Sean answered, straight-faced. "Duncan, let's get to a phone and call in. I don't trust this damn mobile phone today."

"Let me check with the boss and call you back," Jack's hemorrhoid voice said, a half-hour later. "Stay by that phone, and why the hell aren't you using your issued mobile?"

"Damn thing is broken," I responded, while mentally congratulating myself on the wonderful lie. "You're getting good at this, Duncan," Sean said with a smile.

I waited, but it wasn't Jack who returned my call, but Richards.

"O'Finioan," he started, "Hillard told me your visit was anticipated. Now, this is his idea, but I am going to approve it, since you're already in the field. You and O'Shaunessey have the rest of the crew drop you in Huntington where you will combine R&R with observation. Get into street clothes and hit the nightspots. Go to Robby's. You like it there. Rent a car, and save all your receipts this time. Hillard thinks there might be a Mingo County connection. Though frankly, I don't think you'll find out anything in four or five days." He paused, and then went on in the same dead voice, "And sonny, don't do anything that I wouldn't screw."

I was so dumbstruck by his statement that he had hung up before I could think of anything to say. Sean unsnapped the little rubber-coated recorder from the phone's handset and stowed it in an inside pocket.

"Just call it paranoia, Duncan, but I have a strong urge to have on tape anything those two tell me."

"He said he wants us in street clothes for this one. What does he think we're going to do, run around Huntington in combat fatigues?" I asked Sean shyly. "And carrying weapons in full view?"

"You're getting as bad as I am," Sean laughed. "Come on, let's get the hell out of here."

That was how it came about that the two of us were sitting in a posh bar (Robby's to be exact), sipping weak drinks as closing time drew near. We were at a corner table behind a screen of plastic palms and ferns. The only two things we were enjoying were the alcohol and the roll of the waitress's hips as she swiveled among the tables. Sean closed one eye and squinted into his glass. He opened the eye to watch the waitress swirl past, then closed it again.

"You," he said in a low, even voice, "Or we, have acquired an admirer — or grown tails." I looked after the waitress, hoping she would come back.

"Not her," Sean said. "The other one."

The only other person in our end of the bar was a frail-looking kid about my age sitting two tables away. Something pink was in a tall glass before him.

"If that's a tail," I told him, turning back on my stool, "The opposition's is in serious trouble. Besides, he looks more your type," I said, chuckling.

We turned back to our drinks and watched the waitress swivel about, drawing up empty tables. She had just leaned into a booth and lifted one leg high enough to make the view up her abbreviated skirts interesting, even in the dim light, when a high soprano voice beside me said, "Hi fellahs."

Sean looked at me resignedly. "Oh shit. It's a tail," he said. "But not the kind we thought it might be."

"This place is about a close." The voice got a little higher, more soprano. "And you look like you could party all night. Why don't I get some wine and we all go up to my place? It's really close by."

"Duncan?

"Yes, Sean?"

"Did this little cum chewer just proposition us?"

"I believe so, Sean," I told him.

"I can show you a real good time," Soprano was saying. "I've got some good grass to go with the wine."

"The little cock-eater's propositioning us," Sean said quietly, "and offering us pot."

"I do think he is, yes Sean." I said.

The queer's head bobbed on his reedy neck. As Sean got to his feet his eyes widened and a leering grin spread over his face. Then his eyes widened some more as Sean's left hand flashed out and closed over his throat, under the jaw line.

Sean was standing now and the queer's feet were a foot off the floor as Sean pressed him against the wall. His heels began drumming as Sean held his drink in his right hand and took a long sip. Then he set his drink down and scratched his temple with a forefinger.

I turned back to watching the waitress straighten her other long leg behind her as she leaned into a couple more booths. I decided her panties were blue, the pale shade of the queer's face when I looked back at him. His tongue was out and his eyes were bulging. I looked around for the bartender, who was polishing a glass. Sean finished his drink and the bells were playing the William Tell overture as Sean caught the bartender's eye and signaled for more drinks.

"Last round," the waitress said, as she switched the glasses.

"Can you get those, Duncan?" Sean asked. "I have my hands full right now."

"Sure, Sean," I answered. I paid for the drinks and heard Sean say "pot" as he sipped at his drink.

"Four fuckin' hours in a fuckin' pickup truck, a fuckin' International at that, and he offers us fuckin' pot! I could have been sitting at home in a dry county drinking illegal beer instead of riding four hours in a ..."

"Sean," I sipped at my own drink.

"Yeah?" He broke off his monologue.

"Don't you think you ought to let go of him now?"

"Why?" Sean took a long sip of his drink. "He's still breathing." Then he seemed to reconsider and asked, "Where do they throw the trash around here?"

"There's a dumpster out back," the waitress said helpfully, and the queer's eyes got even bigger as he actually tried to smooth a wrinkle on the sleeve of his sky-blue jacket. Then Sean dropped him and his knees buckled slightly, but he caught himself before he hit the floor. He turned admiring eyes on Sean as he rubbed the red spots on his throat.

"You're so strong," he simpered. Sean sighed, then drank, then flexed his body just enough to allow a quick glimpse. I have seen cockroaches scuttle away from light in the same manner the blue-jacketed queer scuttled for the door.

"You're so strong," the waitress said in an imitation of the other thing's voice.

"Oh yes, Sean darling, you are so strong," I said in a half-drunken laugh.

"Kiss my ass," he laughed back. Then a half second later came, "Oh hell no, forget I said that."

"I swear Sean, it's getting so I can't take you anywhere."

The three of us had a good laugh when I said that.

"I'm generally pretty broad-minded about sexual preferences," He said, laughing.

"Yeah, broad-minded," I said as I got off my stool, just a tad bit on the dizzy side, Then I realized the bartender was turning off the lights.

We were up by the crack of noon the next morning. After showering, we collected our rented Dodge and took off for a cruise of the city. On the corner of Halger and 22nd Street, we stopped in for some breakfast. Lots of orange juice and hot, black coffee. On the corner of 20th Street we scored a quarter of pot from a scruff called Chink, even though he was tall, blond and blue-eyed. Seems he used to brag about his adventures or connections in Southeast

Asia till he got the nickname China Joe, and that got shortened to "The Chink." At least this was what we were told by two Huntington city police officers later that day. As with all cops, who knows? I made a mental note, nevertheless, of his location and description and was sure Sean did too.

"It ain't the best," Chink told us frankly. "I suspect it's cut with ragweed or alfalfa, and it's over-cured. But the word came down from the Kentucky boys the goddamned feds were in the area and everybody had to clean up his patches."

I wondered if this baggie had started life as a patch of weeds in a state right-of-way outside of Athens.

"Pressure seems to be on," Sean commented neutrally as we drove away.

Kentucky's native marijuana is a rough horseweed-sized plant that can reach fourteen feet high, but has only about a tenth the strength of the Asian variety. Users refer to it as Kentucky blue, I guess relating it with Columbia gold and red. Sean patted the wheel of the rented car with both palms.

"Aren't you beginning to see a network here, partner? Just of the shadowy form, perhaps?"

"You mean the tie-in between the feds and the drug trade?" He nodded.

"The rumors about the phony sting operations in and around Lexington. The coke parties catered by the state decoys and attended by our big rich governor, or ex-governor, and our big-tit over the hill society." I nodded. Those rumors were so prevalent and so accepted that no one bothered to comment on them anymore.

"And what is the thread that runs true though the whole business?" I just stared at him. For some reason an unraveled thread on the wrapping of one of my swords popped into my mind.

"K.S.P." Sean bumped the wheel with both palms after each letter. "Kentucky State Police." He swung over to pass an Allied Van Lines semi that was laboring up a long grade behind others that had the Roadway and Overnight brands. "Either somebody knows somebody else eager to help a colleague, or somebody is building up points in case he needs a favor in the future."

"A cop," I said.

"A state cop," Sean stated.

"A Kentucky state cop," I defined.

"Yes, but does he call up a drug lord and just pass on the information about a rumored raid, or does he cover himself by calling an Ohio or West Virginia cop to casually mention that we will be operating in his area, and is the other state cop the one who passes the word to the network?"

"The Chink said this word came from one of the Kentucky boys. I took that to be from a cop." Sean pushed out his lips, "It is a puzzlement to me lad, a puzzlement."

Not much was said for several miles. We were each deep within our own thoughts. Trying to make some sense of this crazy world, and this even crazier job that we had. Suddenly Sean looked at me and said, "Duncan, I've been meaning to ask you about your schools. How are they doing?"

"Not too bad," I answered. "The one in Inez brings in the most money, why I don't know, but it does."

"You seemed to have healed nicely." He commented. I knew what he was referring to. The Georgia operation. That was the first time he had brought it up.

"Yeah, well, you know. I have good days and bad days. Although I must say, my good days are starting to outnumber my bad days," I said with a grin.

"Well partner, I have to tell you. When I saw how bad off you were, I had my doubts. I had never seen anyone beat up that bad in my life. I'm just damned glad you made it."

"I wouldn't have made it if you hadn't got there when you did," I told him, and I meant it.

"Hey, what are friends for?" He said, as he passed another semi truck, swearing loudly. A few more miles went on when he got serious and said, "A friend of a friend told me about seeing you with that Mag in your hands a few weeks ago." Oh shit, I thought. "I know that it's still a sore spot for you and will be for a very long time, so I'll make what I'm about to say short and sweet." Sore spot, hell, I was still bleeding. But I didn't interrupt him. Sean was one of the few people I trusted.

"It took more courage to *not* do what you were thinking than to do it. You know what I mean?"

"Yes, I do," I said, and nodded for emphasis.

"Good," he said. "Suicide is for the old, not the young. Now, let us see if this piece of shit car can get us home before supper," he said as he put the hammer down. Those last words would echo in my mind months later. And haunt me for eternity. A few miles down the highway I began to go through our papers, receipts and stuff.

"Sean?" I asked.

"Yes, my friend?"

"Richards wants all of our receipts. Do you think we should give them to him?"

"What do you think?"

I took the handful of ink-covered papers and blew my nose on them. Then I tossed them out the window. Sean laughed loudly as we roared down the highway.

CHAPTER 19

"Clarence is dirty." Jack Hillard's voice came fatally across the table (that's the fucking pot calling the kettle black, ain't it, now). I wasn't surprised. By this time, nothing surprised me about Kentucky's finest. I had seen how helpful they could be if a distressed motorist was driving a Cadillac or a Mercedes. Or if the motorist was thirty-five and wearing a short skirt and a low-cut top. And I have seen what arrogant, overbearing bastards they could be with anyone who didn't have more than the middle class, or was too young to screw. Rumor said they didn't come too young for some. That is one rumor I do believe.

"The opposition?" I asked. (rhetorical question, I know).

"Bought lock, stock, and barrel. He's even making pickups on coal company grounds. We've got the codes from his contact. Richards had him picked up in Prestonsburg and we're holding him incognito."

"How can you do that?" I burst out. The words hadn't even escaped my lips before I realized how really fucking innocent and stupid I sounded. After all, these were the big boys. The big dogs. They could do anything they wanted inside the state line, and most of what they wanted outside the state on an exchange of favors basis.

"First, you identify him," Jack said pleasantly. "Then you roust him and find a few grams of coke or a half pound of hash on him. The coke is easier because the hash is too bulky to plant. You search him in front of a witness, preferably someone who is not in on the plant. I know you're shocked, but that's just the kid in you still. Intellectually, you know it has to be done this way. Besides, we're not framing him for a deal. We only want information on a dirty cop. Now the code is that I call him and say it's Joe from Kokomo. I know it's asinine, Little Joe from Kokomo, so don't comment. I ask him if he can meet the Huntington bus. Now the Huntington bus is the way they used to ship their stuff in, so I imagine it started out as sort of a joke. Little Joe, of course, is four in craps.

"Anyhow, at four in the afternoon, Clarence shows up at the drop site and goes for the package. The package will be hidden inside the door of an abandoned Ford pickup truck down in the center of what the locals still call the Ison's place, even though the coal company bought it years ago and gutted it for a sixty-two inch seam of coal. You can drive all the way up to it in this weather, but if you don't take it easy it's kind of hard on the shocks."

I sipped my coffee and studied Jack's face. He closed his eyes for a moment, and then cocked his head at me. "This contact of his says they've been using the site for over a year. It's just for rush jobs; emergencies. Like when somebody's having a big party and the caterer's afraid of being short supplied. Like when the governor or her husband is in the neighborhood. Happens more often than you think, or more often than they advertise."

"That's high reaching corruption," I said, as I stared at him coldly.

"Proved," he nodded. "And on tape, audio, and video, along with the evidence on the contacts. Clarence may have been out for Noble's suppliers. We're not sure how long he's been dirty. We just know he is."

I thought about trooper Brian Clarence. Like Jack, he was from outside the hills, down around Calloway or Graves County, I think. A whole other world than this one around Inez. As foreign to us as Lexington or Louisville, but in a different way.

"Different kind of people," Jack was saying. "Not like us in any real way. Don't think the same way we do. Just out for the money. Ever wonder how Clarence could afford that big new Tornado on a cop's pay?"

Bucky Noble had owned a Mustang convertible before he

dropped out of high school in the tenth grade. His father's little store had closed that year when the supermarket opened in Inez. Even in the hills an enterprising kid with a bankrupt father can make out financially if willing to work a little.

Bucky Noble had first got my brother into marijuana and LSD. Then Bucky had tried some of his own shit and tried to fly his Mustang to the moon with a ninety-foot cliff as his launch pad. Even with the 302 engine, the Mustang only rose about eight feet above the cliff top. It was a long way down. If Clarence was dirty, he might have supplied Bucky Noble. And if he had, he helped fuck up my brother's life. If he was dirty, he was guilty of the worst crime I knew at that time: he was a crooked cop. Behind him were crooked industrialists and businessmen, crooked politicians and customs inspectors and coast guards and ... I shook my head.

I couldn't reach any solutions except the crooked ones, and we had been hammering away at the coal companies for months now. It was beginning to look hopeless. Money and power is corruption.

"What do we do?" I set my cup on the table and looked Jack square in the eye.

"Not *we*." Jack stood up. "*You*, with my backing and support, of course." He led me out to his unmarked Crown Victoria. It was parked in the shadows at the bottom of the little parking lot next to the lunch counter. A handful of teenagers were hanging around the stairs outside when we went out. "'Bout your bedtime, boys." Jack laughed and then moved away, still laughing. I felt an undercurrent of resistance go through the group like the ripple from a tossed stone into a lake. But they did move off, leaving mutters of "cunt-chaser" and "half-breed" behind them.

My hackles were beginning to rise when we reached the Crown Victoria and Jack fumbled the key into the trunk lid. When the lid opened, the trunk light came on and I didn't need to be told what the long blanket-wrapped parcel leaning with one end up on the fenders was. A long bundle meant a long gun. Jack leaned over to slip the wrapping off and I was looking at a beautiful piece of killing machinery.

Even in the dim light, the blue steel and well-oiled walnut

gleamed. The round eye of a powerful scope shone beautifully at me. I knew the weapon cushioned there in the trunk. Not since the legendary Sharps Fifty Buffalo gun had there been such a piece for civilian use. It was a .475 Weatherby Magnum. This weapon could kill anything that ever walked the face of the earth, and do it in a manner that would leave the user with a sore shoulder or a broken jaw if he was careless in the way he held it.

"I'll make the call," Jack was saying, "And you make the hit. And remember, it's an execution. We take him out and we send a message to the company." That thinking seemed a little faulty somehow. If we set him up, what message would the company get, even if we executed him in their own preserve? By now, they knew we came and went at will. "I'll set it up and let you know when. Remember, all he'll get is the password. If it was clear, it wouldn't mean anything to him."

He lowered the trunk lid with a solid thunk and looked me straight in the eye. "Duncan," he told me, "I hate a dirty cop worse than a diseased whore."

Pot, kettle, black …

"Yeah, either one can ruin a good screwing." I was referring to the screwing we were trying to give the coal company on its coke trade. But Jack just stared at me for a full half minute, and then grunted, "And Clarence is eating crackers in bed."

CHAPTER 20

Five days after my last meeting with Jack, I found myself hunkered down in a mountain laurel patch with the scent of late honeysuckle tickling my nose now and then. I was cramped, hungry, and bored out of my mind. The Kentucky sun on a stripped-out coal seam combined with the humidity of the Appalachians can seem as hot as hot and humid as the Virgin Islands, and what little cats-paw breeze there was didn't dry my sweat. I had enough foresight to add a can of Off to my kit so the mosquitoes and ticks and the damn chiggers (I really hate chiggers) hadn't been too bad so far, and the wasps I had met when I first took position had moved off after a half-hearted buzz or two.

All I needed was a rain shower, I thought, to wash the oil coating off Jack's Magnum rifle and bring out little pinpoints of rust in the hard blue surface. I began to imagine the oil leached out of the stock and the walnut beginning to turn gray. I shook my head and wished I had brought a big box of Kentucky Fried Chicken with me. Then I imagined a big fat juicy cheeseburger and fries from the Dairy Queen. But what I really wanted most was a pint of ice-cold Guinness. But alas, with this, like all things in my life, I would do what I did best; I would endure, and finish the job.

Finally, my thoughts settled in on five days ago. I walked into my house after teaching a sparring class in Ashland, Kentucky, and on my bed wrapped in an oilcloth was the big rifle I now held. Along with the rifle was a typewritten note that said, "Get in some practice shots, and expect a call in a day or two."

So the next morning I took the big gun that I now held over to my Dad's farm. Dad always kept a shooting range behind the barn. It took me ten shots to get the scope where I wanted it, where I knew I could hit my target from almost any range. With this phase of the operation done, I went back to teaching classes and waited for the phone call that came two days later. A muffled voice came over my Inez school telephone. I was told to move in the next day and expect as much as a two or three day wait. If the target did not arrive after five days, abort and wait for orders. The mission was on.

This was my second day in the laurel patch and I felt lucky when the honeysuckle scent came to me. The odor of my own waste products was beginning to pervade my culvert, despite the fact that I had made a crude effort to bury them. It was probably just as well, I thought, that I had only brought a couple of candy bars and some cheese Nabs with me, along with a one gallon thermos wrapped in black tape and filled with water. Then, humorously, I thought of the effort Kentucky's finest would probably expend in analyzing my droppings — provided they were allowed to make a show of effort at solving the execution. I wondered if they would learn what I ate for dinner a week before.

I chuckled to myself and my thoughts turned to friends and enemies and of times long past. Of good times and of bad, but when the first tear rolled down my cheek, I snapped my thoughts back to the here and now. I reached for my dwindling supply of Red Man and pushed a chew into the left side of my mouth, for I would be shooting right-handed. I know tobacco is out of favor right now because it supposedly causes lip and stomach cancer, but as Sean pointed out nobody seems to be studying the correlation between lung cancer and automotive air pollution. You didn't have to look any further than the financial statements of the Big Three to find out why.

Thirty-six hours is a long time to spend in a clump of shrubs barely shoulder high and hardly bigger than the bedroom of a house trailer. Bedroom — that's where I was going to head as soon as this was over. My own or somebody else's. Postpone that. My first stop was going to be a spot that sold food of any kind, and my second would be a shower. Then I would crawl into bed, and rest my head and go to sleep, if sleep would come. I told myself I didn't know what my reaction was going to be.

Always before, there had been the juice of danger to get me high. Here I was, just lying in wait. A simple sniping job that was no more challenging than shooting fish in a barrel — and exactly as dangerous. But why the hell was it taking so long? Why had I been sitting, squatting and lying here in this August sun for damn near three days? How long did it take a dirty cop to get out of uniform and get into regular street clothes, and find the drop site in a neighboring county?

Maybe it was true what they say, I thought. They like them dumb. And believe me, I had met some dumb ones. These thoughts and many others were going through my mind like a whirlwind when I suddenly froze all movement. From the corner of my vision, two hundred yards away from me, a man's shape was standing back among the sweet gums. I had no way of knowing how long he had been there. I calculated no more than three to five seconds, but he was obviously studying the area.

His medium-gray clothes were about as good as woodland camos in the shadows. I took a full ten minutes to get back into my shooting position. The rule is, movement attracts the eye, so if you must move, do it as slowly as possible. Good thing I was fairly good at T'ai Chi.

Now that he was there, I had no trouble following him as he stood, looking slowly over the area, then moving back to view it from another angle. I watched him for a full forty minutes before he dropped behind the ridge to the east. A half hour later, I heard a car engine start up. The boy didn't trust somebody! But he must have felt satisfied that he was safe because his blue Bronco crept up to the edge of the clearing about ten minutes after the engine started up.

When he stepped out, he took another slow look around, then walked to the center of the clearing.

He spent another ten minutes going over the rocky soil and staring at the weed growth. Finally, I realized what he was searching for — skid marks! Helicopter skids can leave definite or faint tracks, according to the weather and the pilot's skill or style. Most try to touch down flat with the whole skid, but some will rock slightly backward so the rear end touches first. They are the ones that mangle a tail rotor. Others tilt slightly forward as if studying the ground. That's what is meant by style.

Clarence may have been hoping to identify this pilot by his skid marks. When he couldn't find any in the center of the clearing, he began to walk in an unwinding spiral, each circle nearer the edge. He seemed to be frowning as he circled past me, and his hand was hovering back near his hip. He kept dividing his attention between the ground he was covering and the old Ford truck door. Finally, his circle took him too close to the trees for any sensible pilot to land and he turned and stalked directly to the stash.

Nobody from the hill country pokes his hand under a largish piece of sheet metal without taking some precautions. Funny things with teeth and scaly things with fangs and rattles sometimes hide under them. Clarence's precautions were simple. He took the door by its old-fashioned, turn down handle with his left hand and had his pistol in his right. He was standing back as far as he could while still being able to reach the handle. He flipped the door over and jumped back, his revolver ready. All he saw was the little sign I had left more than two days earlier. Surprise! was all it said. He was beginning to look either puzzled or worried when I shot him.

The big Weatherby round isn't quite as thick as the forty-five bullet, but it's designed for penetrating things, like human flesh, so it travels several times as fast through the air. I heard the big bullet whine as it ricocheted off a rock and screamed away over the woods after passing through my target. Clarence wasn't going anywhere, so I took a couple of minutes to police my culvert, cleaning up candy bar wrappers and Red Man packages, and stuffed them in my kit.

With everything except the rifle dangling from my left hand, I walked coldly up to the body. My bullet hole was right where I had set the crosshairs — five inches below the top of the big man's breastbone. To make the message clear, I fired two more rounds into the corpse, each shot entering under a nipple to form a perfect triangle. Clarence's body heaved some as each of the soft-nosed rounds mushroomed in the hard earth beneath it.

I drug out my cleaning rag and began wiping down the big rifle as I headed home for dinner. The outside of the rifle was all I cared about. It was Jack's rifle — or one he had either borrowed or stolen, and I damn sure wasn't going to leave my fingerprints on it. It was Jack's worry from now on.

There was a ripple in town when the queries came in from London state police about trooper Brian Clarence. Women in three counties had called demanding his whereabouts. Seems he was missing appointments. When his wife called in, she was told he was probably somewhere resting. She retold the story and Jack repeated it.

Two days later a call came in from the coal company office. One of their pilots had spotted what appeared to be a body while on a routine check of their land holdings. Routine check, my ass. He hadn't bothered to land because the winds in the area were tricky and a thunderstorm was fast making its way into the area. Yeah, right.

I read later that trooper Brian Clarence "had apparently tripped over an abandoned truck door and accidentally killed himself with his own service revolver after going into the remote area for target practice, something he was frequently known to do." His wife, four girlfriends, and a coal company executive attended the funeral. The youngest girlfriend and the widow sat on each side of State Police Detective Jack Hillard. It made a lovely picture for the papers.

CHAPTER 21

Two months after the hit on Clarence, Sean, Jack, a uniformed trooper and I were riding a Jeep Cherokee over a stretch of the rough, weather-beaten road of an abandoned strip mine (strip mine, here we go again). I had to keep my window rolled partway down because of all the cigarette smoke coming from the front seat. But I was enjoying the crisp fall mountain air, and it was helping to keep my head clear.

Something was wrong. I could feel it. I couldn't put my finger on it, but it was there. The feeling you get down deep in your gut when you know something is about to go terribly wrong. I almost voiced that feeling, I wish to God I had. But I had been trained to carry out an assignment to its end. No fear, no looking back.

Snoopy was telling me one of his stories. Snoopy was my nickname for Sean, and he always liked to begin his stories with a description of the night. And the night was always dark and stormy. I used to find that stock opening amusing. Then Sean pointed out to me that good literature, whether it's grand opera, the Bible or a comic strip, has varying levels of interpretation. At one level the dark and stormy night was what he called the "sturm und drang" of the soul. The storm of the soul. He had been referring to that idea a lot lately. Then at other times, he would wonder aloud why mankind ever invented a soul in the first place.

The Church, he could understand. Sean believed they had invented the soul originally to account for the difference in a live body and a dead one; something was gone, so they posited a soul.

And what was gone was the breath. The heart beats on for moments after breathing stops, so the loss of breath must stop the heart.

He would ramble on, usually after an assignment. Sometimes his ramblings would take on the tone of his true intellect, that of a genius, while other times it was almost childlike. He had cracked earlier that the Mafia pays better, and he asked aloud to himself, "What the hell are we doing here?" He had been brooding over that for ages now. Not the pay, but the assignments. "What were we hired to do?" he would ask.

"To deal with drug lords who are above the law because of money, power, or respectability," I would recite.

"Polly want a cracker?" would be his wicked retort. As I sat there with Sean in the backseat of that rough-riding Jeep, I kept wondering, what in the hell was he doing? Why were we having this conversation now, with Jack Hillard and another state super trooper riding up front? Was he trying to pick a gunfight with them, or was he trying to prove a point?

"That's what they swore me in for," I told him. "To go outside the law to get people who are known to be guilty, but the law can't touch." I have to admit that I had been having doubts about some of our operations. A thousand dollars a week somehow just doesn't go as far when you are twenty-five as it seemed like it ought to when you are twenty-one. Sean seemed to read my thoughts. "How can an assignment where you are shot at fail to be worth more than one where you buy a couple of joints or a hit of coke from a street dealer?"

"You know the pay for the safe run helps balance out the dangerous ones," I told him. "As for big shots, what about that hacienda we cleared out in Guatemala, and the two in Bolivia? And the fields we burned in Honduras. All the big shot houses."

"A tad removed from Jack Hillard's jurisdiction, wouldn't you say? Those big shots were all far from the green hills of Kentucky. But they are as dead as the nearest hillbilly. A forty-five or a shotgun is impartial. You pull the trigger and it goes bang! No matter at whom it is pointed."

"We've taken plenty of the opposition off the streets."

"The opposition, yes. The opposition, of course." He paused and closed his eyes in a way I had learned to recognize as a force to make me think.

"Did you ever pause to think we might be removing competition? It can give one pause." With each statement, his voice was becoming more venomous. Damn him! There it was. The rodent that had been gnawing at the back of my mind was all at once thrust through into plain sight, shot before his den and hung up on the wire fence for a passerby to see — and to smell — after a couple of days.

The idea was hung up full-blown for me to stare at and sniff around. I guess a thousand dollars a week can turn the eyes and nose away from a lot of things when you are very young. But Sean was older. The older brother I had always wanted. He should have seen through them. After all, he was … he was Sean!

"You know," he was reading my thoughts again. "I believed in them at first. You believed good old Jack up there because he cultivated you and your family, and we trust our friends. I believed them the way I believe that the way to meet force is with greater force. I studied sociology a long time ago, but I could never get past the idea that there's a law, and then there is what people do. And after that there is what people who are sworn to enforce or uphold the law do.

"The whole point is not unlike the story of the Baptist preacher caught in the whorehouse where he tells his deacon 'Do as I say and not as I do and you'll get to paradise.' Remember how you snickered and felt superior the first time you heard that joke? I know I did. That's the way the joke works. What gives it its humor."

From the front seat, Jack turned and glared at Sean. Then he clamped his lips shut in a smirk. The uniformed state boy driving the Cherokee never let his eyes waver. He reminded me of a side of beef — lean-muscled and carefully dressed to USDA standards. He also reminded me of another rat bastard I had waited for, for a very long and uncomfortable time.

Sean looked into Jack's eyes, and it was like watching a snake stare down a rabbit hole. Jack's eyes were bold at first, then wavering. Then there was something that looked like triumph — a gloating — in them, as if he had us right where he wanted us. When Sean spoke, it was in a lazy voice and was part of a line from Shakespeare.

"There comes a time in the affairs of men … "

"Ok, you know the drill." Jack's shitty little hemorrhoid voice cut in. "You've seen the maps and the satellite photos. You know this land. Don't let them see you, but make sure they know later that you've been there."

There was a two-mile hike in front of us. Tall, fat Jack seemed to have developed a fondness for that two mile drop off point. It probably gave him time to run to the nearest restaurant and get a cup of coffee and screw the waitress, or jerk himself off, while we were doing our recon.

Reconnaissance with prejudice. That's what Richards liked to call these operations. And this one brought us home. Or almost home. My first time out had been a simple buy in Paintsville; my worst had been the child-killing episode in the coalfield. This operation was but a few miles from both of those sites, overlapping the county line of Martin and Johnson Counties.

We circled our target. This time, it was a large mobile home, once used as an office and left when the coal operation closed down. One thing you don't do on a recon is let your partner get too far from you. All cars are gray in the dark and everything that moves may be an enemy. You pray not to kill the wrong cat.

One sentry was on an outcropping high above the road. I caught him against the stars and sent Sean after him. At this time, Sean had moved up from the garrote to the ice pick. He had decided the garrote took too long. Earlier, he had disallowed the knife because it caused excessive bleeding, and he hated to be bled on. This time, I stood by with my MAC-10 ready as he worked his way back and forth across the slope. There was nothing for me to see once he was five paces away.

Then, incredibly, the guard lit a cigarette. I could see the glow on his face as he sucked on it. Finally, he flipped the butt over the edge of the outcrop and it made a falling arc as it dropped the thirty feet into the forest floor. Then there was a faint scuffling sound on top of the rock, and a sound like a bag of feed falling. I had stood stock-still for perhaps ten minutes when I felt a touch at my elbow. I was backed up against a tree at the time, so the touch was not threatening.

"Want an Uzi?" Sean's voice whispered in my ear. "Recently confiscated with extreme prejudice."

As I said, I'd come full circle. We were back after our old enemy, the coal company. A hundred yards from the abandoned office trailer was another one of those bulldozed flats made up mostly of broken rock and clay. We knew the helicopters had been flying in again, but we weren't supposed to try and stop them. We wanted to see who met the chopper and try to identify them. Infrared photography had been suggested, even automated photography. But we had been told the equipment was not available at this time. Just like a lot of shit we needed but never got. Like night vision!

I had a feeling we were about to see some familiar faces if that chopper dropped in. The ones you see on walls and telephone poles just before Election Day. Anyway, we were about to take out the guards, then see what we could learn about the chopper and especially about who met it. If they were feeling especially cocky, there wouldn't be too many sentries. The fewer people who see you, the more easily they're accommodated for, or disposed of. One down and no telling how many others to go.

One we found a hundred yards from the big trailer. Since he wasn't isolated like the one on the rock, we circled him and did a triple circuit of the base to make sure there weren't any others. When we were absolutely sure, I waved Sean back and went in for the barehanded kill (a very, very foolish mistake on my part). This one was wearing a forty-five and I had to keep him from drawing it.

The idea was to get a chokehold from behind, disarm him and break his neck. I had used this technique before with no problems. I was getting nervous, because a sliver of moon was beginning to peek through the trees on the ridge to the east. The guard was standing on an old prospector road, the kind they gouge out while looking for workable coal seams, when I took him.

Maybe my timing was off, maybe he moved. Hell, he might have even heard me. The next thing I knew, we were rolling around on the ground. I had managed to shuck his gun out of his holster and clamp one arm around his throat. We thrashed about in the scrubby pine seedlings that had begun to cover the grade. That young son of a bitch was tough.

We rolled over the edge and fetched up against some larger brush. I still had his forty-five in my right hand and my feet were tangled in pine branches. I kicked my feet loose and he clawed for my eyes. Then he managed to clamp onto my throat. Finally he began to weaken, and I shuddered in one ragged breath before I heard the sound.

The next seconds are still a jumble in my mind. Oxygen deprived as I was, there was no mistaking the sound of a shotgun slide jacking a round into the chamber. I went off-guard in a reflexive dive and flung the captured forty-five up and felt the hammer fall on an empty chamber. The stupid shit was carrying an automatic unprimed! I was rolling and working the slide when the shotgun roared.

I never knew where Sean came from, nor why. My eyes were still blurred when the twelve-gauge split open the night. The moving figure that gave me time to ready my weapon was Sean O'Shaunessey. Somehow he had gotten between me and that twelve-gauge blast.

The blast threw him across the guard I had been trying to strangle. As the shotgun's slide jerked back to eject the spent round, my reaction was automatic. I fired three rounds into the third guard's chest. I brushed dry pine needles off my face and struggled back on my feet to where Sean, his face blown away, lay across the guard's chest.

The guard's face was dark in the thin moonlight. He was rubbing his throat and looking happy to be alive when I grabbed him by the hair of his head, put the gun to it and pulled the trigger, emptying the magazine. The whole mess had been caused by him fighting me. Sean had been right again. An ice pick to the heart or brain would have been easier.

I picked up Sean's captured Uzi and moved a few yards into the shadow. There was no need for me to signal. The gunfire had done that. Ten minutes later, the Kentucky State Police came nudging their four-by-fours over the prospector road. There was some commotion over at the mobile home, and a distant swoop-swoop-swoop of helicopter blades, but I didn't even raise the machine pistol.

There was no longer any question of reconnaissance and discovery. The whole assignment was blown to hell. As I fondled the cold steel of the Israeli weapon, one thought forced itself into my numbed mind: I had bet my life we'd miss no sentries, and it had cost Sean his.

CHAPTER 22

Coming down from the aborted surveillance assignment was harder than anything I had ever yet done. I was stunned, in shock, almost walking in a coma. My weapons felt like strange materials distributed about my body. They no longer had the feeling of being old friends, just dead weight.

When the helicopter had dropped in and lifted Sean's body off toward Frankfort, I was placed in the Jeep Cherokee and headed for debriefing. The Cherokee was a silent tomb except for the purr of the engine and the crackle of a wrapper as Jack opened a fresh Hershey bar. Then the sugary odor of Swisher Sweets blended with the foul odor of milk chocolate. I swear the son of a bitch had kept his nose up Richard's ass so deep and for so long he thought he was Richards. Chocolate mixed with tobacco smoke, I was fucking sick of it!

I dozed and woke, expecting to hear some comment by Sean, some of his private little essays on the meaning of existence as applied to such groups as the Unicorns, who do not exist. Or the members who do not exist. Through my wanderings, Sean's words came back to me. Phrases I had taken as bravado assumed new aspects. Phrases like "blaze of glory," "meteor strike" and "die a hero" all merged into the solemn cant of a preacher my mother had once taken me to hear. In fifteen years, the ignorant preacher's words had not reoccurred to me. Now they did with an awful and awesome meaning that made me want to crash my fist into the polished metal of the jeep's doors.

"Greater love hath no man than this, that he lay down his life for a friend." I knew Sean was gone when he didn't read my mind, take up that thought and twist it into something amusedly sacrilegious. It probably would have been something to do with laying down a friend's wife, if I knew Sean.

Yes, the huge silent stalker was gone. There would be no more all-night, all-day drinking sessions in Huntington, or Boston, or Mexico City, or anywhere. It occurred to me that everybody was dead. The person in the farmhouse, the little girl, her rapist. A dozen other assorted men and women. The ridiculous little colonel in Guatemala, Nancy, her brother's family, the men in the warehouse, the young half-trained Unicorns, and now … Sean.

Sean, who had put the Unicorn team together from assorted odds and ends of talent. He had gotten his blaze of glory, and it was one that promised to haunt me until I resolved the guilt I already felt. The guilt of having overlooked that last sentry.

"O'Shaunessey was suicidal." Jack's hemorrhoid voice came from the front seat, and was followed by the fucking odor of sweet tobacco smoke and milk chocolate. "He was good, but he was suicidal. You could see that. Me, I'd have just shot that third guy."

Right then, after his comment, I snapped. I took the Uzi that Sean had taken off the sentry that he had killed and punched Jack in the back of his head with the front end of the barrel. Hard (I learned later that it took six stitches to close the gash). I had snapped.

"You mother fucking, son of a goddamn bitch!" I growled. Jack howled in pain and the uniformed trooper driving the Cherokee tried to draw his gun and keep the truck on the road at the same time.

"No!" Jack yelled at him and grabbed his hand. "He'll fucking kill us all."

"Give the asshole a cookie," I said, as I moved to the center of the back seat so I could watch them both. Or shoot either one; I didn't give a shit right then.

"You." I pointed the business end of the Uzi at the driver. "Both hands on the wheel and fucking keep them there."

"Damnit, Duncan … " Jack tried to say something.

"Jack, unless you want your fucking head blown off, keep your shitty mouth closed." My words came out cold as steel, and I meant every one of them.

Jack moaned and cried over the gash in the back of his head, but he didn't speak another word until we were in Lexington. Damn good thing, too. I was suddenly very tired of Jack. I realized I had been for some time. And I was tired of all this stalking and spying, tired of easy arrests and bloodbaths, tired of the stench of gunpowder and the odor of blood. At twenty-five I was burnt out in the only career I knew of that would pay a high school dropout a thousand dollars of untaxed money a week. Just for killing people ... And sometimes dying.

"Today is a good day to die." The phrase came back to me from my reading about the Cheyenne. But not for Sean to die. Sean had been too vital, had enjoyed life too much to be cut off at ... I suddenly realized I never knew Sean's age. I also realized I might never know unless I read it in the newspaper. That, I knew would never happen. I finally fell into a half-doze, that state of consciousness where you can sleep lightly but still be aware of your surroundings. I came out of it as we were pulling into Lexington.

When the short and ridiculous debriefing was over, I was sent immediately to the company shrink. What a fucking joke! This shrink decided I was suffering from shock and depression brought about by excessive bonding and identifying with the late victim. He recommended three things — rest, women, and booze — the things I had months ago, told him, I always went for following an operation.

He didn't seem to notice that this was a different kind of operation. In this one, we had failed. No. *I* had failed. I left his office, walked to my motel room (which was one of our safe houses) and curled up with a bottle. From my window I could see University of Kentucky coeds swinging past, and at any other time I might have drifted up to McDonald's, Hardee's or Arby's and tried to meet one or two. Now, I just wanted to explore the depths of the fifth of hundred proof I'd brought with me.

I finally gave it up as a bad job. Those are times when the mind refuses to succumb to alcohol, and I was in no mood for a woman. I ended up walking Lexington's streets that night. Up and down Limestone. Southland Drive to Circle Four. Then out East Main to Lexington Mall and back to Meadowthorpe on West Main. A couple of Metro cruisers doubled back on me a few times — I assumed to make sure they were not being cut out on any dope deals. They didn't come close to me. Damn good thing too, I wanted to kill anything in a police uniform.

I wasn't worried about surveillance at the time. That would come later. But that is another story. On the way back to Meadowthorpe, I glimpsed the military section of the Lexington Cemetery with its rows of small marble crosses, then the high shaft of the Henry Clay monument. Reflections on this brought back the Holbrook kid's words, "The people down in Lexington have their priorities straight. Two foot high crosses for men who die for their country and a hundred foot column with statues for a fucking politician." A member of Sean's four groups of organized crime.

As I walked back over the bridge spanning the railroad tracks, I heard voices. That reminded me that there were night roosts for Lexington's homeless between stays at the shelters. One man's voice said, "Are you gonna give it to me?" And a woman's voice answered, "Not without a rubber." A second man's voice laughed and said, "I told you, she ain't drunk enough yet, Carl."

I resented the bums. I hated them because they were alive. And all those I cared for were dead. When daylight came through a red dawn, I made my way back to McDonald's. The late October days had brought the migrant workers into town and the hustlers who called themselves labor contractors. A few farmers in dusty pickups or old station wagons were still choosing their workers. I needed action, but I didn't feel eight or ten hours of hoisting seventy-pound sticks of tobacco over my head was going to release my tension. A couple of pert coeds began giving me the eye, but I wasn't interested. They had been eyeing every lonely-looking man in the place, and there are plenty of those around September and October.

I drank coffee until the place cleared out, then walked back to my room to shower and change. Fuck shaving. I dawdled and when I finished it was nearly time for Richards to be in his office. When I got there, he wasn't alone. It appeared that Detective Hillard had stayed in the Bluegrass, too. When I presented myself and was identified through the intercom, Richards precise herringbone voice said, "Send him in."

I thought that was wise because I had fully intended to go in, either past or over the bespectacled male secretary who sat at the intercom. Richards and Jack were both behind Richards's desk, pretending to go over some papers. When I walked in, Jack pretended to flick an imaginary mote off the paper and Richards looked over his gleaming glasses.

"How's the headache, asswipe?" I said, as I looked Jack straight in the eye.

"Enough along that line." Richards said, as Jack's hand went to the back of his head, which was now covered with a thick bandage. "What's on your mind, Duncan?" he asked.

"The funeral," I answered.

"What funeral?" Richards asked.

"You know," I replied, with a sinking feeling. "Sean's. Sean O'Shaunessey, co-captain of the Unicorns."

"Sean O'Shaunessey," Jack mused. "Wasn't that the name of that John Wayne character in Ireland?" I pointed a finger at Jack.

"How would you like me to finish the job?" I asked coldly.

"I have no such recollection of any such character," Richards said mildly. "Are you sure you're not making him up to pull our leg? And just what are the Unicorns you are referring to?"

I unzipped the duffel at my feet and tossed the two loaded magazines across his desk. "You can have these," I told the pair, and sent the Ingram after the magazines. "And this." The issued forty-five skittered across the desk and into Richards lap. He glanced at it coldly and turned his attention back to me. Jack sat looking at the loaded Ingram on the desk with fear in his eyes. Richards bit off a piece of candy bar and fumbled out a cigar.

"I know nothing of anyone named O'Shaunessey," Richards said. "Nor of any group called Unicorns. The young man seems overtaxed and distraught," he added to Jack.

Then I went over the desk, faster than I had ever moved in my life. The snub-nosed forty-four, which was in my back belt, sprang into my right hand as I pressed it against Richards too-big Adam's apple.

"How would you like to eat *this*, you fucking son of a bitch?" I asked him, as I pulled the hammer back. He just stared back at me. Then I was facing more federal marshals than I had even seen at one time in my life. And wherever they had materialized from, each one was holding a loaded three-fifty-seven Magnum and each one was pointed at my head.

"You sorry-ass rat bastards," I said, as I dropped my forty-four on the desk and was manhandled to the door. Down the marble stairs and into the lobby they hustled me. At the spot that used to be the post office entrance lobby, three of them shoved me against the wall while two more kept weapons pointed at me. They then proceeded to beat the living shit out of me.

When my arms refused to rise to my own defense, they hustled me out the door and down the front steps. I remember the snap of the American flag in the wind as they hurled me out onto Barr Street. A passing Wildcat Cub swerved to avoid me as I fell to the asphalt.

My life as a Unicorn, I thought, was over.

CHAPTER 23

I sat in the middle of Barr Street, a few yards from North Limestone, and tried to let my head clear. I was alone, unarmed and unemployed, except for my pitiful excuses for karate schools. When my head was straight enough, I heard the American flag above my head snap in the breeze again. For some reason it reminded me of the flag that flew above Black Kettle Tepee before the Sand Creek massacre.

I looked up and an empty-faced Metro mounted policeman was watching me from atop a sleek brown gelding. Perfect pair, I remember thinking. No balls on either one of them. Brakes sounded on my left and I looked that way to see a Wildcat Cab looming over me. The driver got out and came toward me with a look of genuine concern on his face. He put out a beefy hand and hauled me to my feet. Then he turned and yelled to the cop, "Hey Officer, this boy's obviously been assaulted!"

The cop wouldn't hear him and instead turned his horse onto Church Street, turning his back on me.

"You got mugged, boy?" The taxi driver wanted to know.

"Yeah," I told him. "Mugged by a shitload of marshals for asking when my best friend's funeral was going to be held."

"Marshals, huh?" The driver was edging away as if I had said Gestapo. "I always thought they were okay. I know you don't ever want to let metro get you in the elevator by yourself, but I thought the feds were straight."

"They're all just a branch of organized crime," I quoted Sean to him. Right now I felt like killing something, but my bruises told me I had better get into a hot tub and soak for a couple of hours before my muscles knotted up. Jack Hillard and Richards had joined Ponytail on my list.

Hell, when you're twenty-five and have seventeen confirmed killings to your credit, a hemorrhoid, a crooked cop, and a bloodless bureaucrat don't look too impressive even if you are unarmed. Sean didn't exist. Never existed, according to Jack and Richards. The Unicorn team had never existed. The drug busts, the raids, the killings had never happened. A quotation from Sean popped into my head. A title, really, of a play by some old Spanish playwright: La Veda es Swino.

As the stars and stripes snapped smartly in the air above the narrow strip of lawn in front of the federal building, I had a feeling that life is more than a dream. With the DEA against me, and every fucking cop in the country and the rural Mafia, my life was almost about to become a nightmare. Hell, Duncan, I told myself, and felt the empty holster in the small of my back. Your nightmare started the day Jack Hillard drove into Inez. Maybe you're just now beginning to wake up.

Maybe the Lexingtonians have the right idea. Maybe basketball is more important than safety and security, honor and honesty. I watched the cab from the company named after a basketball team drive away. A couple of bearded, scruffy men and a greasy fat woman edged around me as they made their way from the Horizon Center on Martin Luther King to the Community Kitchen on Upper Street. Maybe they had the right idea. Free meals at the Horizon Center, medical attention and clothing at the Community Kitchen and the Salvation Army to sleep in or the bridges to sleep under.

Hell with it all, I told myself. I'll stick to what I know, what I do best. What I was damned good at. I headed for my motel to collect the rest of my gear. I was going back to my schools and the legitimate work I knew best. I was going back to Inez (but not to stay long). But more, I was walking into the mouth of hell itself.

EPILOGUE

A month went by and one cold Monday morning I walked into my Inez school and opened the locked drawer to my desk. Atop my ledgers and receipt books, I found a plain cardboard box. My first thought was a damn bomb! But some instinct told me no. Still, I unbent a coat hanger to pry the flaps open from behind my desk. I used the hook end to lift out what I found there. Lo and behold, my old familiar snub forty-four Magnum.

I flipped open the empty cylinder and looked down the bore, thoroughly cleaned and oiled. I wondered if they had fired a few rounds and saved the bullets for use in any convenient shooting they wanted to pin on me. I decided I was paranoid. But then again, maybe not.

Two months later at two-thirty in the damn morning, I was awakened by the ringing of my telephone.

"Who are you and what the fuck do you want?" I growled into the mouthpiece. Richards voice came back at me.

"Duncan, we're putting together a new squad and it needs an experienced captain." He said this with no preamble.

"Richards," I said. "Fuck off." I then put the receiver next to my ass and farted, then hung up the phone and went back to sleep. After that, my life really started going to hell. I survived three attempts on my life, one by knife, one by group attack and one by shotgun. My schools suddenly started losing money and I ended up bankrupt, with the bank getting a quarter of a million dollars worth of equipment for a two thousand dollar loan.

Then one of Jack's old judge buddies put a hundred thousand dollar full cash bond price on my head for a non-appearance on a day his office told me no cases were scheduled. This was after Jack arrested me with the help of two other cops with weapons drawn. He then demanded ten thousand dollars cash to let me out and pay off the two thousand dollar bank loan that was included in the bankruptcy. This was the way I found out that the Kentucky courts are little mirrors of the Supreme Court. Whatever they quote is the law of the land; whatever they deny does not exist.

A while back, I passed through Harrodsburg and spotted just what I would like. On a hill above Highway 127 sits what appears at a glance to be a well-preserved Sherman tank. I would like to chug up Limestone Street and press the main barrel to the area windows and blow Richards all the way to hell. Then a tanker of fuel later, I would like to roll up to the courthouse and blow it all the way to hell.

Sean found his blaze of glory. I am still dreaming about mine. But what can I say? I am not suicidal, my tendencies are otherwise directed. If I survive getting this book in print, I would very much like to tell the rest of the story or join the Irish Republican Army. Either way, I'll still be fighting for my life and freedom.

I lost my Dad a few years back. The doctors said it was a heart attack. I'm just not sure about that. That seems to be happening to a lot of people these days. People who know things, who question. Rest in peace, Dad. Part of me went with you.

I must say, I have changed considerably since my life as a Unicorn. If you guessed I no longer live in Kentucky, you guessed right. You see, I had enough gray matter left to get the hell out of hell. Pun intended. But some things in life never change.

I have been under constant surveillance since that night, long ago, when I told Richards to fuck off (and farted in his ear). Taped telephone calls, intercepted mail, cars following at discreet distances.

I guess what they say is true. Once a player, you can never quit the game. For some strange reason, I see a final showdown brewing here. If that is the way it must be, then so be it. But remember one thing: I was never broken as a boy, and I swear by God, you will never break the man!

Well, it's now December, 2011. Damn what a mess things are in. The more things change, the more they stay the same I guess.

Get ready …

ABOUT THE AUTHOR

Robert Duncan O'Finioan is an author and martial artist. Born in 1960, he was taken at a young age by his parents and delivered to a secret government program known as Project Talent, a sub-project of the notorious MK ULTRA Program. The program used severe trauma to split his personality into several alternate personalities, one of whom was trained and enhanced to become a Super Soldier known as Omega Unit 197.

It was only as an adult, after years of missing time, blackouts, odd experiences, and terrifying nightmares that a car accident restored some of Duncan's memories of involvement in these secret programs. Duncan had also recently learned of the existence of three distinct other personalities in addition to 197.

Today, Duncan, along with his partner, Miranda Kelley, continues to be an outspoken advocate of bringing light to these programs and getting them to stop. No child should be tortured against their will, and certainly not by programs run by the very people who are supposed to protect them.

DuncanOFinioan.com
DuncanOFinioan.wordpress.com

11214197R00093

Made in the USA
Charleston, SC
07 February 2012